FORGEMASTERS OF THE REALM

THE ELVEN TOMES

SNÆBJÖRN

Order this book online at www.trafford.com
or email orders@trafford.com

Most Trafford titles are also available at major online book retailers.

Printed in the United States of America.

ISBN: 978-1-4669-9765-3 (sc)
ISBN: 978-1-4669-9764-6 (hc)
ISBN: 978-1-4669-9763-9 (e)

Library of Congress Control Number: 2013913249

Trafford rev. 07/22/2013

 www.trafford.com

North America & international
toll-free: 1 888 232 4444 (USA & Canada)
fax: 812 355 4082

CONTENTS

DEDICATION

I wish to dedicate this book to Charlotte Elizabeth Brown, member of our family who has been of EB since birth. I call her Charlotte's Web, from the famous book, because she will always be wrapped in gauze for the rest of her life; though she was cocooned in a spiders' web. Epidermolysis Bullosa (EB) is a very rare genetic skin disorder. It is a horrible disease where she cannot make skin on her body and is always getting infections. She is incapable of regrowing new skin, making her subject to cancers and such. Charlotte will never become normal; her condition is almost fatal, and rarely will persons with EB reach their fifteenth birthday. Not only do new parents of an EB baby have to instantly learn medical procedures and the lifetime care of an extremely fragile child, they also have to overcome an overwhelming grief for the loss of their dream of having a perfect and healthy baby. EB is a treacherous, horrible monster! It causes such devastating pain and agony. Please contact the EB Medical Research Foundation if you wish to donate time or resources to help the victims of this dreadful disease. I intend to donate my proceeds to this worthy cause.

DebRA of America
16 East Forty-First Street, 3rd Floor
New York, New York 10017
212-868-1573

To Charlotte, I wish you the very best in this world, and I hope you will enjoy my writings because the small things in life can be the best things. I always write about hope, honor, and righteousness in my writings because without hope, nothing else matters. If the worst case happens, I will someday meet you in Valhalla if the gods wish it to be.

ACKNOWLEDGEMENT

To Sylvia and Tomas Tomasson, thank you for the times you helped me when I was down and out.

KAFLI:

EPISODE ONE

The Department of Homeland Security (DHS), which had been established in 2002, took over as the protective body of the citizens. In the year 2002, with the blessings from Congress, the DHS initiated the Implant Policy. In essence, this required all citizens to be monitored with a tracking device. Political figures argued that due to the escalation of "man-made disaster" activity—code words for terrorist doings—they needed to do something "for the children." They also decreed that all religious organizations (including chapels, denominations, or church meetings) must submit any speech regarding religion. The Arabs, on the other hand, had no such restrictions (other than the Implant Policy) placed upon them.

During the Great Disaster of 2014, the government launched massive assaults against homegrown rebels. Due to the use of chemical weapons, the countryside was left devoid of people. It was estimated that 60% of the population of the Earth had perished as a result of the Great Disaster. The president, Barry Tathhaus, declared martial law and appointed czars for the government departments. One of the appointed was Janet Lygari as the first head of the DHS.

Most of the populations that escaped the Great Disaster clustered around the major cities as security and safety were of paramount importance. As a result, travel restrictions were placed upon the population, with the DHS constructing force-fences around the surviving cities. The people then needed to get permission from the DHS to travel about or even to meet in groups of five or more. The DHS constructed underground speed-rails to connect other surviving cities, with the cities all setting up their own force-field fences. Ordinary citizens were banned from owning or operating a vehicle; only first-response employees could travel via an automobile. News organizations could only broadcast approved journalistic material. Citizens could not own businesses; they could not engage in any activity where profit was made. Of course, all the political leaders were exempt from such regulations. Such was the state of the world, building a community "for sake of the children." Books were burned, and the only ones used in the schools taught an approved history of mankind.

The lawlessness around Joldugrof, the residential area, was astounding. Gangster activity was up by 70 percent as the neighborhoods relied heavily on gangs for security. Eighty percent of the residents were black, and of that, 55 percent were unemployed. Crime was rampant—there were murders, rapes, robberies; home break-ins were the daily norm. The police didn't patrol the area, and when notified of a crime that had been committed, they were slow to respond. The legal system was overwhelmed, the prisons were overflowing, and the politicians were blind, mute, or oblivious. The rich or political "ins" all had armies of private security companies around them. The blacks, Arabs, Latinos, Russians, and the poor people were unemployed or just not interested in working. They turned to crime because the welfare provided by the state required documents or requirements for work. Eighty-five percent of children born were from unwed parents, or they didn't even know who their fathers were. The dropout rate was astounding, 70 percent, and those did graduate could hardly write or read.

Our hero, if we can call him that, was a struggling archaeologist, a white male, unmarried, and living in government-subsidized housing—what we call a slum. All the government's programs were useless unless you were of European heritage, and trying to get benefits that the government promised was like getting your teeth pulled. He was dejected about life; he couldn't find a girlfriend; he wasn't gay; he was unemployed as an archaeologist; he didn't have a brother, mother, or father; he was miserable. He never succeeded in anything—not in high school or college. He wasn't a sportsman and was never very popular. Perhaps it was because of his looks. Growing up was hard too. He was always picked on because of his looks. His ears, looking like they had been pinned to his skull, slanted toward to the back of his head. He had an impish look about him. He wasn't very tall—kind of short, really—and not muscular. He wasn't ugly, but he wouldn't be crowned the best looking in class either. In short, our hero was a nondescript nobody, and he knew it too. His brother, mother, and father had been killed in the attack on Augusta City when the terrorists blew up the Trade Center. He not seem to have a defined purpose in life.

I suppose that our hero, for all practical purposes, was at the end of his rope. He was full of ambition and promise when he first moved to Joldugrof, but no longer. His apartment was burglarized five times in the last six months; they took his computer and archaeological supplies. He dared not venture outside the apartment after dark. He had been robbed twice, stabbed once, and suffered abuse at the hands of the blacks in the neighborhood. He even tried religion but found it so impossibly stupid. *Where was this God when we needed him the most?* This "Love thy neighbor" nonsense was for mainstream America, not for the demons who ruled the neighborhood.

Thusly have I penned this story, written for the trodden and the hopeless in this life, the mistreated inhabitants in this world. This is his tale, perhaps fictional. But what if it isn't fiction?

Chapter 1

The Parcel Deliveries

The alarm clock was buzzing as if afire. The sleepy young man sat up and swatted the clock until it stopped chiming. He didn't sleep very well last night. It was always the same old nightmare. It was so realistic—the greenish hulk with huge canine teeth that extended from its lower jaw and over its lips. There was also the dark hooded figure of a man reaching out with an arm that ended with scrawny fingers and fang-like fingernails sent chills down his spine. Forgetting the nightmare, he yawned and stretched his arms. He detected the foul odor of bad breath and cupped his hand over his mouth, still yawning. *Well, that didn't do a thing to relieve the stench,* he thought. Staggering like he had too much to drink, he made his way into the kitchen (which was also the living room) to make some coffee. His tiny flat badly needed repairs. The paint was peeling on the walls, the stick furniture had been repaired often in the past, and the single lightbulb hung from the ceiling gave his apartment a cheesy scheme. He turned on the coffeepot and turned and headed to take a shower and brush his teeth.

After his shower and tooth brushing, he took his index finger and dragged down his lower eyelids to inspect his eyes. He splashed some Old Spice aftershave lotion on his face, and he felt somewhat refreshed. Because he was without a beard he had no use for razor blades. *Kinda like Indians, I guess. No beard,* he declared. Returning to the kitchen, he poured himself a cup of coffee and turned on his transistor radio; his cell phone, television, toaster, and radio had been stolen in the last break-in. Adjusting the radio by turning to the right and the left until the reception was best, he listened to the news and the weather report. *Another day in hell, I guess.* Then he heard a low knock on the door. *Who could that be?* He grabbed a knife from the kitchen table. "Yeah, what do you want?" shouted our hero.

"Parcel for you, sir. I'll leave it at the door," said the unseen male voice on the other side of the door.

He looked out the peephole in the door and could see the back of a man descending the steps. He tightened the grip on the knife and undid the five latches on the door. He peered outside with the door slightly ajar, and on the floor was a parcel. He scooped up the package, redid the door latches, and then inspected the package. "Hey, it's for me," he said; the name Anthony Ragnarsson was printed on it. Anthony tore the package open and inside was a letter, a cryptic note. "What the . . . ?" Anthony said as he read "Meet me at 3:00 p.m. in the park. It will change your life." There was no name or signature on the note, which left Anthony puzzled. *Three o'clock in the park, eh? Right. As if I intend to show up there, especially if I don't know who is going to be waiting for me,* surmised Anthony. *Change my life? The only thing that can change my life is a darn job.*

Anthony finished dressing and tidied up his tiny apartment. He needed some things from the corner grocery store, but as he had little money, he decided to pick up only some coffee, bread, and milk. *Sucks to be poor. Hope I have enough food stamps to cover 'em,* Anthony thought. As he left his apartment, he spotted cockroaches clinging to the wall. *God, I hate this place. Vermin swarming everywhere,* reflected Anthony.

The complex he lived in was a dilapidated three-story brick structure. He lived on the third floor with an apartment to the right and left. The occupants of the room on the right were black and had no father figure. The family had six children, and the mother was probably about fifty years old. Their youngest, a male of about thirteen years old, was a known crack dealer. His sisters were probably whores; numerous unknown men were scurrying about at all hours of the night.

The rooms to the left housed a family of Hispanic origin, who never talked to anyone. Anthony didn't know what the man of the house did for a living, but at least, they were still living as man and wife. Their two children seemed to be smart . . . or at least, managed to stay in school.

It's a waste of time talking to the super about the roaches. He wasn't even interested to hear that my apartment had been broken into five times, mulled Anthony. The odor from the stairwell reeked of vomit and urine.

Anthony left the building with a feeling of relief. At least he could get some fresh air. He had to constantly look around, especially in this section of the town. *Rule. 1: A black person is safe when walking around. Two of them, be extra vigilant. Three or more, they are a mob; cross the street or turn around,* reflected Anthony. The sidewalk was littered with empty beer cans and trash. What used to be automobiles along the streets were now just hunks of corroded, stripped steel. He turned to the right in the direction of the Latino sector. At least there, the grocery stores were safe. To the left was the black section, and if anyone who went there wasn't black, well, they were taking their lives in their own hands. Every old shop in that part of town was burned down from the race riots in 1995. The windows and doors of the newer shops were barred, and they only let five customers in at a time.

Ten minutes later, Anthony was in the Latino section, which was a relief. The grocery store was right ahead, and the first bus stop in the area was about five blocks farther down. The taxi cab companies and the public buses didn't operate in these sections of town. That meant going through the gauntlet of the black, Latino, Russian, and Arab gangs when he was employed just to get to work. After he had picked up his groceries, he had to travel back to his apartment, clutching his precious booty from the store. He finally made it back to his rooms, bolted the locks, and put away his groceries.

Anthony turned on his radio just to have something to hear.

The voice on the station said, "This is a public service announcement from the DHS."

Great. Another useless comment from the government, Anthony thought.

"Everyone needs to be vigilant. If you see or hear something, report it. Every citizen has a duty to report any suspicious activity. Contact your nearest DHS unit, local police, or contact any government official. This has been a public service announcement from the DHS. We now return you to your regularly scheduled programming."

This is total nonsense. When have they EVER done anything of consequence to deal with the man-made disasters? questioned Anthony. *Who in the world makes up these words? "Man-made disasters." It's like the government can't or won't deal with calling people terrorists.*

At 2:30 a.m. the next day, Anthony woke up in a cold sweat, screaming. He grasped his head with both hands. His heart was pounding like a jackhammer. "Argh. I . . . I must be crazy, going out of my mind. What the hell is wrong with me?"

stammered Anthony. It was the same old nightmare, only much worse this time. He felt like his body was paralyzed from fear. The green thing was back, only this time, with a knight. Anthony thought it was a knight. It was dressed in full black armor and stood with a huge sword between its legs. It wore a helmet, but the eyes within it weren't eyes—they were orbs of lava, no eyelids, no nothing. It just stared at Anthony. It did nothing more, just stared.

And then the scene changed. There was the hooded guy rapping on Anthony's window, beckoning Anthony outside. The fingernails were scratching on the glass, like someone running their fingernails on a chalkboard. Anthony needed a moment to reorganize his thoughts, get his heartbeat back to normal. He nearly leapt out of his skin when he heard a scream from a cat in the alleyway below. He crept out of bed, turned on the lights. *That's better,* he thought. He went into the bathroom to take a pee and then washed his face with cold water. He went into the kitchen to make some coffee, and when it was percolating, he heard a noise at the front door. He ran to the drawer, and he clutched the biggest knife he could find in his hand. "Who's there? I'm armed, and I'll hurt you if you try to get in!" yelled Anthony. Dressed only in his shorts, he stood back from the door and shouted a warning again. "I'm warning you!"

"Parcel for you, sir," said the unknown person at the door.

"What the . . . ?" exclaimed Anthony in shock. "It's three o'clock in the morning. Nobody delivers packages at this hour of the day!"

"I'll leave it at the door," responded the stranger as he scurried away from the door.

Anthony didn't know what to do. Open the door and be surprised by another robbery? And at this time of the morning, stuff didn't add up. He crept up to the peephole in the door but saw no one. He ran his hand through his hair, still uncertain as to what to do. The coffeepot was singing, indicating that it was ready, so he got a cup of coffee and sat at the kitchen table, facing the door with his weapon in hand. "I must be losing my mind. NO ONE gets packages delivered at three in the morning!"

Anthony just sat at the kitchen table, drinking cup after cup of coffee. It was about five in the morning when he finally mustered up courage to investigate the door again. There was no one who could be observed through the peephole, so he quietly undid the latches and put a foot against the door and peeked out. He found no one, but like before, he found a package on the floor. He scooped the package up, latched all the locks, and put it on the kitchen table. Using the knife he had in his hand, he sliced open the package. Inside was an envelope and a copy of yesterday's newspaper. Inside the envelope was one thousand dollars in hundred-dollar bills and a letter that read

You never showed up yesterday, so here is one thousand dollars to prove that I am sincere. There is an article that I have circled; please read it. The money is yours to keep. Just give us a little bit of your time, and regardless of the outcome, keep the money.

"Hmm, strange indeed. And again, no signature, no nothing," Anthony muttered under his breath.

He retrieved the newspaper, flipped it open to the article, and began to read it. "A magic shop, of all things. A stupid magic shop," muttered Anthony. God knew he needed the money; he decided to visit the shop.

The Majick Shoppe

At ten o'clock the next day, Anthony was waiting in the security checkpoint in the sub-rail station for transportation to HearthGlen. He had to wade through the scanners and answer a myriad of questions. The DHS goon, a black guy, said something that he didn't quite catch.

"I axeted a qeston. Why ya wanna go there? Bizness or pleasure?" asked the DHS thug.

This clown needs to speak English, not Ebonics, thought Anthony. "I have a job interview in HearthGlen," he replied.

The security guard squinted an eye. He seemed to be sizing Anthony up. "'Kay, you can go" muttered the guy toward Anthony. Anthony followed the railings lined with pronouncements from the DHS and TSA (Transportation Security Agency) about man-made disasters and shadowed fellow passengers until he reached the boarding station. The ride took about thirty-five minutes, and Anthony disembarked, found the information desk, and asked for directions.

The attendant asked what the address was, so Anthony fished the newspaper clipping and showed it to him. Looking around, Anthony saw several TSA agents toting submachine guns stationed here and there within the depot.

"Ah, yes, let me see now," responded the attendant as he keyed in the address in the computer. "Ye Olde Majick Shoppe. Here you go: 1974 Carry Road. You need to catch a bus just across from the station here," instructed the attendant as he pointed toward the exit.

"Thank you, sir," said Anthony.

The bus station had about fifteen buses waiting for passengers to embark and disembark. The buses all looked the same: grimy things with screen mesh over the windows. Anthony asked which bus went by Carry Road and he was directed to bus number 15. The bus ride took about an hour, and out of habit, he scanned the street, looking for people who looked like they were in a group of three or more. Then he realized what he was doing. He felt relieved to be in a safe area of town. Anthony headed in the direction of the shop, which was five blocks away. Suddenly, a swarm of unmarked cars converged on what appeared to be an abandoned building. He knew from his experience that it was the FBI and DHS agents. He wouldn't stick around to answer any questions as the agents rounded up the occupants of the building. *Not my problem. Probably deadbeats anyway,* thought Anthony.

Anthony opened the door to the building. Stenciled on the window was "Ye Olde Majick Shoppe". A chime somewhere in the shop piped up when the door opened. Inside were three people, apparently employees; they were rearranging the shelves. "Hello," said Anthony to the middle-aged woman at the desk. "I'm looking for someone, but I don't know who," stated Anthony as he handed the newspaper clipping.

"Ah, Mr. Ragnarsson, good to see that you have arrived. If you can just make yourself comfortable, someone will be with you shortly. Please, browse our wares if you like," said the receptionist with a smile.

Anthony perused the inventory of items, such as fermented spider eyes, nether warts, ghast tears, and beakers for brewing potions and mortar and pestles. Of course, there were books on magic, DVDs, and magazine subscriptions available as well. The ceiling of the shop was rather unusual: it was higher than normal ceilings and was cylindrically shaped, with stars on it. He couldn't imagine that this line of business was rather profitable. *But not any less than archaeology,* he thought. A sign hung on the wall said Psychic Readings. *I guess this is what a magic shop looks like. Never been in one before,* surmised Anthony. *Kinda dingy. Wood floor, cheap paneling.* He felt a tap on his shoulder, turned, and found a cute young lady facing him. She was probably twentyish—perhaps twenty-five—with long golden hair, and she was the same height as Anthony. Her baby-blue eyes were captivating, blue as a swirling whirlpool. Her nose was like a button but not too large and not too small. Her lips were perfect. "Follow me please," she said as she escorted him to the back room.

"Can I ask why I am here? I know absolutely nothing about why I am here, and I have never seen anyone here whom I know," said Anthony.

"Ah, yes, of course. Uh, my name is Lillian by the way. We wish to make you an offer that will change your life. Other than that, my companions will fill you in on the details. But of course, you are free to leave at any point if you don't like our offer," said Lillian. She opened the door, held it so Anthony could pass through, and the door slam shut after they entered the hallway. On the right and the left were five doors, all of them closed, and at the end of the hallway was another closed door. The shop was deceptively large; the hallway must have been fifty-five feet in length.

As Anthony and Lillian were halfway through the hallway, the end door opened and an old man stepped through. He was immaculately dressed, had gray hair and a well-kept beard, and sported a black cane with a huge jewel on the top. "Welcome to our enterprise. I am Harald, and I will be conducting the interview with you," he said. He extended a hand while Anthony said, "Yes, you obviously know my name. But I am a loss. Is this a job interview? What kind of interview?"

"Lillian, excuse us. I hope that you will see much of her as these proceedings progress. Come in, come in. Our offices are rather comfortable," said Harald.

Harald seemed to be well-educated, and his dress spoke of money. Harald escorted Anthony into the room and was invited to a comfortable large plush seat. Harald returned to his desk, rummaged through the drawers, and finally said, "Got it. It seems like you are an archaeologist. I can't imagine anyone making lots of money in that field. What kind of archaeology do you do?"

Anthony tried to size up Harald. Not many people had so much money—at least, no one he knew of who flaunted it the way Harald did. "I've done a bit of digging around the pyramids in the south but mostly taught some night courses for the local schools," answered Anthony. "Why all the secrecy? If you wanted an archaeologist, you could have advertised for one. Kind of an odd way to hire someone. I mean the odd letters and knocks on the door, don't you think?"

Harald chuckled and with a large grin said, "Ah, you see, there is a pesky obstacle called government. The less they are involved, the better. I'm sure you will agree with that."

Anthony smiled and wryly said, "Ugh, the government. We can always do without it. If I may ask, what is the pay?"

"Oh, you need not worry about the pay. We have plenty of funds for the projects we have in mind. What kind of pay are you looking for?" replied Harald.

"Well, I need shifting screens, strap sets, ropes, trowels, shovels, measuring tapes, brushes, kneepads, squeezes, air blowers, and dental picks to start with. All of my tools were stolen a while ago," explained Anthony. "That takes money and plenty of it. And as for me? Oh, I was thinking something around the area of thirty thousand dollars a year."

"My word, my young lad, you underestimate your value. I was going to offer one hundred and fifty thousand a year," Harald chimed in with a laugh.

Anthony's eyes grew big and his jaw dropped when he heard that. "One hundred and fifty thousand dollars a year? That's unheard of! There must be a catch here somewhere."

Harald cleared his throat and said, "Of course, there are expenses, all paid in full, and of course, we supply your archaeologist's tools. The only catch is that you keep quiet about what you are doing, and NEVER divulge your employer."

"Well, I certainly will honor your wishes. What exactly are you looking for anyway?" responded Anthony. "Oh yeah, do I have any help in this?"

Harald mused for a moment and responded, "We wish to excavate around the old ruins of Vokva and Jarnsmiða and look for dwarven artifacts. I have a professor of antiquities who will go with you, if you don't mind. There is so much that has been lost over thousands of years. It will be a very educational and satisfying work, I can assure you."

"Indeed, sir, I would love to have a crack at it. When do we start? And Vokva—isn't that in the zone where people aren't allowed to go into? What about travel and work permits?" queried Anthony.

"Well, that is why I offer good pay. I have no problem getting you to Sanctuary City, but we need to smuggle you out because of the restrictions by the government. One good thing out of this is that dwarven artifacts give a hefty reward because no one is allowed there. Good! Here is the name and address for your partner. As for permits and paperwork, leave it to me. You can start whenever you are ready," thought Harald. Harald scribbled down the name and address of Anthony's partner, one Amber Strickland, 1005 Jasmine Drive there in HearthGlen, and gave it to Anthony.

Anthony read the note and asked if he could use the telephone to contact Amber as his cell phone had been stolen. Harald blinked his eyes and said, "No, sir. We do not have a telephone. I did not put her telephone number because I prefer you contact her in person. Secrecy, you know. Telephones are not very secure contraptions; talk on the telephone and you may as well shout from the rooftops. She will be waiting for her partner to show up, so it won't be a surprise when you show up."

Anthony was pleased about the bonuses and excellent pay, but he wasn't pleased about going to a forbidden zone. People have been shot trying to leave their zones. *What happens if I get caught in the middle?* reflected Anthony. *I better take care, something stinks here. Dwarven artifacts?*

Partnership

Anthony arrived at 1005 Jasmine in HearthGlen the next day at eight o'clock. At least she wasn't living in a slum. She had a nice place. It was not luxurious, but it was a nice and good neighborhood. He used the knocker on the door, and after rapping several times, he waited for an answer. The occupant who answered the door was stunningly beautiful. She had shoulder-length bronze-colored hair, a perfectly well-shaped, proportioned face, with luscious lips. She seemed to be about the same age as Anthony, and she wasn't wearing a wedding band either.

"Good morning, ma'am, my name is Anthony. I was supposed to meet Amber—Ms. Strickland, I mean. Is she available?" asked Anthony.

"I am Amber, please come in. You must be the digger who was supposed to show up."

Anthony blushed slightly and thought to himself, *WOW, what a catch! Hope she isn't queer.* After he entered her home, Anthony was pleasantly surprised by the works of art hanging on the wall and the awards Amber had received for her work. There were certificates from several countries, as well as her graduate degree from the university. She seemed like a very intelligent woman, which was a trait he admired in the opposite sex.

"Wow, you seem to be very in tune with the world. You are quite the globe-trotter, which I am not," commented Anthony toward Amber.

Amber blushed lightly and said, "Thank you. Perhaps you can teach me a thing or two about archaeology someday. Follow me into the kitchen. I'll make a pot of coffee. That is, if you drink coffee. I can offer other things to drink if you wish."

"Coffee is just fine. A touch of sugar and some milk in it, please." Anthony smiled. "And please, do call me Tony."

"Tony it will be then," Amber said as she grinned, "and coffee with sugar and milk it is. How did you ever get into archaeology? It must be dirty work, digging holes and such."

Anthony watched Amber make the coffee, put the milk and sugar in the cups, and dance back to the table to wait for the coffee be finished. "Well, I was always interested in ruins, even as a kid. I always wondered what it was like to live in those times and places. Not to mention the wonderful works of art, I noticed that you have a lot of paintings on the wall. Are any of them originals?"

"Unfortunately, no, but I do love art," responded Amber.

"Do you have any sisters or brothers?" queried Anthony. "My mother and father were killed in the attack at the Trade Center. Unfortunately, I never had any brothers or sisters."

Amber paused for a few seconds, as if she was deciding how much, if anything, she wanted to divulge. "I have one brother. He lives in Smarihetja. My parents live here in HearthGlen." Amber was sizing Anthony up, trying to figure out what made him so appealing. Obviously, he was intelligent but not afraid of work. "Coffee is done," she said as she strode to the pot and filled the cups.

Anthony was stricken by Amber's baby-blue eyes. He watched as she blew away some loose bangs from her eyes and sipped the fresh coffee. "How much do you know of this Harald? The owner of the magic shop, I mean. I've only met him for about half an hour, and just the one time."

Amber smiled, and the slightest dimple showed up. "Gee, I was going to ask you the same question! Like you, I've only met him once, in person."

"Wow," uttered Anthony, "he obviously has money, but other than that, I know nothing about him. I met him in the strangest way. He sent me two letters with the weirdest messages. All I got was a newspaper article that had been circled. When I found out that it was a magic shop, I went, just out of curiosity."

"Tony, I had the same letters," Amber said as a wry frown fell upon her face. "Do you have any idea what we are going to do? I was told that we needed a professor in antiquities and dwarven artifacts but nothing else. And the money he offered was extremely high for it."

"Well, I at least found out where we were going. He told me that we are going to Vokva and Jarnsmiða, which is in the Forbidden Zone," responded Anthony with astonishment as Amber listened. "Something here doesn't add up. How can the owner of a magic shop have so much pull with the government, getting permits and permission to travel? And then we would need to be smuggled out. People have been shot for trying to go into the Forbidden Zone."

Amber pursed her lips and frowned. "Now that I think about it, you are 100 percent correct. Something smells fishy to me too."

Anthony nodded in agreement. "Well, perhaps BOTH of us need to go back there and demand some answers from Harald. What we DON'T need are any legal problems or any other kind of problem. The government can make our lives miserable, to say the least."

"That sounds like a plan, Tony. Should we meet there in the morning, nine-ish perhaps?"

At 8:45 a.m. the next day, Amber and Anthony met outside the shop. They talked about which questions they really needed to be answered so that they could avoid nitpicky ones. They agreed that they needed to have a unified front before facing Harald. They entered the shop, and Harald was working the customers' desk. Amber spotted three male customers, but they looked out of place, not customers looking for wares. Harald caught Anthony's eyes, and with a roll of his eyes toward the three strangers, he quickly shook his head as to say no.

"Good morning, sir. If you need any assistance, please do ask," Harald spoke loud enough to let the other customers hear him. Anthony hooked an arm under Amber's and whispered, "What in the world is that about?"

Amber put on a childish face and started laughing. Whispering back, she asked, "Am I overacting?"

They were around the section where the eyes, ears, and tongues used for making potions were located, and Anthony picked up some pickled eyes. "Hey, honey, take a look at these," Anthony said, keeping an eye on the strangers. She poked an elbow at his arm and muttered under her breath, "Not at all, 'honey.'" to which both of them laughed. After a few minutes, as they eyed up Anthony and Amber, the trio left the shop. Harald waited a few minutes, walked outside to ensure that they were gone, and came back inside and motioned Amber and Anthony to follow him.

"What was all that about? And you better have some good answers or we won't accept your offer," stated Anthony firmly.

Harald smiled and said, "As I said previously, secrecy is the key. You haven't heard—I mean, about the trains?"

Amber shook her head to indicate no and then asked, "What about the trains? I know that every now and then, the trains are down because of maintenance in some parts of the city."

"My dear lass, the latest delay wasn't for maintenance. It was a man-made disaster. Terrorism, to be precise. They always come into the stores pretending to be customers. They are government agents. They are snooping around, hoping to hear about something or someone out of place," explained Harald. "Please, come into my office and I will answer all of your questions."

Lillian brought in an extra chair and offered refreshments, returning soon with cups of coffee and cakes. "Now, what are these questions you have for me?" asked Harald.

Anthony broke into a question with, "For what exactly are you looking for? I don't believe that you are looking for dwarven artifacts, so don't try that one again. How can you possibly have access to travel permits *unless* you are *with* the government or *in* the government? And lastly, you wouldn't have to smuggle us out, unless this plan was without the government's involvement. Something doesn't add up. Are we being set up for some sinister plot?"

Harald assumed a worried face and said, "What I said was true. I was hoping to obtain some dwarven artifacts. But more importantly, I want some books—a set of books, really. I am not a conspirator of either the government or the terrorists. The books

I seek are from millennia ago: the tomes called *The Book of Knowledge*. Because I have no interest with bungling politicians or the government, we must smuggle you out of the city. I have contacts with rebels from the outside to help us smuggle you out. I have money, plenty of it, so it is easy to obtain the necessary permits. Now, are you satisfied?"

Amber jabbed Harald with acidic questions. "No, I'm not satisfied. You claim to be a neutral party. Who in the hell are you then? What do you want with these books? How do we know that you won't be killing us off when you get them? I want some serious answers!"

Anthony nodded in agreement with the questions from Amber. "How do you know that this book or set of books exists? What is your interest in these books? *The Book of Knowledge*—what kind of knowledge is contained in the book?"

"Tut-tut, my young friends. I can assure you that the books are real. I know much more than you can suspect. As to who I am, Harald is my name, perhaps someday you will know more about me. I wish to recover the books to safeguard them. To whom they will go or where they will wind up is not for you to know. Regarding your safety, I can offer you assurances that you will come to no harm, now nor in the future," answered Harald. He opened a drawer and withdrew an object wrapped in linen. "Perhaps I can persuade you with this." He offered it to Anthony.

Anthony then unwrapped the object and exposed a silver cross embedded with precious gems. Etched on the cross were Nordic runes. It was obviously valuable, and he blew a whistle between his lips.

"Do you have a magnifying glass?" uttered Anthony. Harald gave him the magnifying glass and he began to pore over the object. "Seems real . . . but it would have to be tested. Flat on the back, but still, the gemstones must be worth a lot. Amber, what are these runes along the spine?"

Amber wrote down the runes on a piece of paper, and after a few minutes, she translated them. "Seems like something about Traikon and the key for salvation. Odd. Something about a Keeper," she whispered.

"What is a *Traikon*?" Anthony asked Amber.

"Gee, I don't know. Harald, do you know what it is?" quizzed Amber.

"Nothing I know of. Maybe a god or something. Anyway, I know it is very valuable. Just the gems and exquisite workmanship makes it rare indeed," replied Harald.

Anthony chimed in and asked, "Where did you get it? I've never seen anything like this."

Harald cleared his throat and said, "It's been in my family for many generations. I recall my great-grandfather talking about how it came from the Blafjall Mountains."

Anthony handed the artifact back to Harald and said that the object needed studied to authenticate its age and origin. "I'm not sure of this quest of yours, not just for a book. The cross is exquisite, but you haven't answered to my satisfaction. If you aren't associated with the government and you are not a rebel sympathizer, then who do you work for? You are obviously not a collector of antiquities, so what or who are you? The government leader Janet Lygari can have us shot just for being around the rebels."

Harald frowned a bit and said, "All I can do is offer you safety while in my employ. Perhaps someday you will know everything about me. If you agree to the quest, I will depart without the cross, you can keep it and any other artifacts you find. I only want the books."

Anthony gazed at Amber with a shrug of his shoulders. "Can you excuse us for a moment? I'd like to huddle up with Ms. Strickland and get her opinion. I'm not sure if we will agree to it, but I'm not declining either."

Harald smiled, and his face lit with hope. "Surely. Of course, I will. Can we offer you some more coffee and cakes? Take all the time you need."

Amber and Anthony sat knee to knee as they discussed the cross and its inscriptions. Anthony was not convinced that Harald was forthcoming, but he couldn't get the cross out of his mind. Amber too found it discomforting that the answers were clouded with intrigue, but the Norse runes made it real to her. Amber seemed to enjoy the drama, the tinges of danger, and the unfound relics to be uncovered in the future were enticing. Anthony, not a he-man by nature, had doubts about the dangers in the Forbidden Zone. But Anthony liked Amber, and he hoped that they would be working together. They finally came to an agreement, voted yes to the quest, and summoned Harald back to the room.

The Train

Both Amber and Anthony were packing their bags for the trip. Neither of them had ever been to Sanctuary City, and they were looking forward to the journey. They didn't have to bring any supplies with them as Harald would equip the party. They were reminded that secrecy was of utmost importance, and Harald suggested that they travel as a vacationing couple, newlyweds perhaps. They were booked into the Regency Hotel and were to be contacted after they settled there. At any rate, the two of them didn't want to be burdened with luggage, so they chose to only take two suitcases each.

Anthony was saying good-bye for the moment to his dingy apartment. *I won't miss you,* he thought. *I am so glad I will not have to put up with the puke, the urine in the stairwell. Now the neighbors—if only they would move out, then it would be livable.* He mused about the crumbly neighborhood, the crack houses, the prostitutes, and the thugs. The world would be a better place without them. Sirens pierced the air from downstairs. Another raid. It seemed to Anthony that he was the only one in the building who hadn't been arrested, jailed, or interrogated for hanging with cohorts or rebels.

Amber was waiting at the depot, craning her neck to see if she could spot Anthony. Most of her luggage contained reference materials on ancient languages and what little had been known about Vokva and Jarnsmiða. It seemed that the inhabitants of both areas just disappeared The government didn't want to teach about history, or the English language for that matter. The only thing they were teaching were government-approved lessons. All that was left were just ancient ruins of castles and fables about the dwarfs and elves in the area. Of course, they were just stories made up by uneducated people. What those people couldn't understand, they just made up stories for. Interesting reading for their entertainment value, however. She eventually found Anthony trudging toward her and dragging the two suitcases in hand. "Good morning! I hope you enjoyed your sleep, Tony. I'm really looking forward to the trip."

Anthony slapped a smile on his face saying, "Amber, great to see you again. I didn't sleep very well last night. Guess it is because this is new to me. Here you go, I got your tickets," as he relinquished her tickets. "I hope those stupid TSA clowns don't give me a hassle. I brought the cross with me. Hope I don't get roughed up for it."

They entered the line for the security checkpoint, and soon, a TSA agent was perusing their tickets. "You two are in the wrong line. You need to go into that one. That one is for prechecked passengers."

They toted their entire luggage, and with that, they entered the other line. There were no hassles, no questions, and the TSA agent even ordered up a luggage carrier to help them. "VIPs, now that's service," whispered Anthony to Amber with a laugh. The train was an older model with wire mesh coverings on the windows, but that was standard today because of the rebel activity. When they boarded the train, they were escorted to the sleeper section where they could travel in comfort. It wasn't a very large sleeper—just two bunk beds—but it offered some privacy. The room was fitted with a sound system that played soft music. Soon the train was in motion and picked up speed, rocking gently as the cars traversed the tracks.

Comfortably situated, Amber and Anthony felt awkward as their eyes met. "Tony, do you want to be on the bottom or the top?" asked Amber.

"Y-you can, um . . . uh, can be on the bottom," Anthony said as he blushed. "Oh my, I'm sorry. I didn't mean it like that."

Amber put on her dimpled smiley face and suddenly started to laugh. "Well, we were told to travel as a couple."

Anthony turned red as a beet and laughed as well. "Let's go to the dining car, grab a bite to eat. Then we can figure out how we are going to cohabitate!"

They went to the dining car and ordered two steaks with several mixed drinks. They chatted for a bit as they were enjoyed each other's company, laughing and talking about each other. Every car was secured with two TSA security guards toting submachine guns. However, it wasn't long before Anthony and Amber accustomed themselves to the presence of the guards. The food was excellent, and the alcohol in the drinks loosened up their tension. Soon they were speaking as if they had known each other for years.

Suddenly an announcement came over the speakers. "Passengers, we regret to inform you that your trip will be delayed for approximately one day. There is unexpected maintenance on the tracks ahead, so we are diverted to another track to Fort Hermana. I hope you haven't been inconvenienced."

"Well, first glitch on our travels," said Anthony between sips off his drink.

After the meal, both Anthony and Amber wandered throughout the train. It wasn't a tour because of the covered windows, but it did take the monotony out of the journey. They had both relaxed to the point that they could enjoy the presence of each other, whiling away the time in conversation. They talked about "the zone" in hushed tones, lest someone would overhear and report them as rebel spies. Anthony enjoyed his profession. He always was interested in historical things. Although he confessed that he liked the excitement of doing daring and banned things, he was uncomfortable with associating with rebels. He wasn't much of a daredevil.

"It has been a pleasure to have you as a partner," said Anthony, and he added, "Should we get some shut-eye? We should be arriving Fort Hermana by the morning."

Amber beamed and suddenly gripped Anthony's arms and kissed him. "Yes, that sounds wonderful," she breathed.

Anthony became light-headed by the kiss as he was totally startled by it. Amber was the first woman who displayed any affection for him, and he loved it. Anthony and Amber, hand in hand, returned to their car, laughing. Anthony was enthralled by Amber's presence, but not wanting to offend her, he decided to take it slow with her.

It was about 2:00 a.m. when Anthony heard a hustle at their door. He couldn't sleep very well because of the kiss earlier in the day, and he was trying to make sense of it. *Rap-rap.* He heard a muffled sound at the door and the sounds of feet scurrying away from it. Anthony, puzzled, cracked the door open, but no one was there. He scanned the car hallway but saw nothing until he looked down toward his feet. *Strange,* thought Anthony. Before him was a small shoe box. He retrieved it, closed the door, and examined the heavy box. Inside was a derringer and a handwritten note that said "You will probably have some use for it." Mystified, Anthony pocketed the derringer, deciding not to let Amber know about it as it would probably upset her. His eyes turned toward her, and he spent a few moments just staring at her sleeping body. *Harald better keep his word about our safety, but if not . . . ,* thought Anthony as he patted the derringer in his pocket.

At the breakfast table room hours later, Anthony and Amber enjoyed their coffee and engaged in small talk. "I guess we'll be stopping soon, and then we will take a different set of tracks going to Sanctuary City. It'll be a three-day journey from here. I'll be glad to arrive, see the sun, and get fresh air again. Too bad we can't take a look at Fort Hermana. There were historical events that took place here."

Amber smiled fondly toward Anthony and added, "And we can take in the sights too once we reach Sanctuary City. Maybe we will have some time to visit the Diplomatic Sector. I hear they run tours around there. I really enjoyed our first night together as 'newlyweds.'"

"I guess we'll have to find another way to get to Fort Laekur. It is just military base now. I wonder where we can find our escorts." Anthony beamed. "We shouldn't talk about our work until we arrive in Fort Laekur." He was struggling over the matter of the derringer but decided not to bring it up. More importantly, he was worried about running around with rebels.

The rest of the trip on the way to Sanctuary City was uneventful. Finally, they had finished the first leg of the trip, and they were hoping to grab the June sunshine and fresh air. There, it seemed that between the FBI, DHS, and TSA agents, law enforcement personnel were everywhere. There were teams on every block of the city, apparently because of the high number of rebel attacks from the countryside around the city. Anthony and Amber joined the tour of the Diplomatic Sector, which was interesting in itself. In the Diplomatic Sector, the government had posted guards dressed in ancient garb and armed them with lancers. It was obviously done for the tourists, and Anthony and Amber enjoyed posing for photographs with the guards. They stopped by an outdoor café littered with umbrella-topped tables where they stopped and ordered iced teas. "Not bad for a vacation spot," said Anthony. "Nice. The Diplomatic Sector, I mean. I can't say much about the other sections of the city though."

"Tony, my darling, you are too cynical. And to think that we are on our honeymoon." Amber laughed.

Anthony noticed a waiter walking toward him with a note in his hand.

"I have been instructed to give this to you," said the waiter.

Anthony perused the note and then asked, "Who wrote this?"

"The gentleman over there," the waiter said as he turned around, pointing. "He's gone now."

"Never mind. Thank you for giving it to me though," Anthony said.

With a puzzled look, Amber asked, "What's on the note?"

Anthony, deciding not to speak aloud, whispered, "Take a look at it."

On the note was a simple sentence: "You are being followed. Someone other than you is looking for the book."

Their vacation had come to an end. Reality took hold of Anthony and Amber as they decided to go back to the hotel and wait for their escorts to Fort Laekur. As they were leaving the café, Anthony patted the pocket where he had placed the derringer. *Now I'm worried. Harald has some explaining to do. Either he has told someone about the book, or he has spies among his company,* thought Anthony.

Both Anthony and Amber stayed in their hotel for the meeting with Harald or his company. They spent the time discussing the mysterious note, and both of them vowed to interrogate Harald when they meet again. Anthony was bound and determined to not let any harm come to Amber. "If someone else is after the books," asked Anthony, "then maybe it won't be safe to go any further?"

Sanctuary City was a small city. Its fencing was visible throughout the city. They checked in at the Regency Hotel and were given a room on the first floor. On their way to the hotel, the volcano Eldfjall could be seen from the distance beyond the bay, shrouded with ominous dark clouds and thunder and lightning. But it was no ordinary lightning storm—the streaks of light were racing among the clouds, not striking down toward the earth. They also seemed to radiate from a single point, not moving around as normal thunderstorms did. It seemed to Anthony that they had taken a part of an ill-omened journey.

Chapter 2

Fort Laekur and Surroundings

The staff of the hotel went through their check-in procedures and explained the usual security requirements for their stay. "No picture taking in any place in the city. Do not approach the air force base, it is a restricted area. It is unlikely to occur, but if the city comes under attack by the rebels, there are shelters throughout the city," briefed the check-in man. "It seems that you have chosen a rather strange location for a honeymoon. But I wish you a comfortable stay."

Anthony thanked him and added, "Is the volcano always this way? I mean, the cloud covering and the lightning?"

"No, sir, it only started acting strange about three days ago. I've been here forty-five years now, and I've never seen it like that before," replied the man at the counter. "But not to worry, it is too distant to be a threat. It is across the bay."

The couple settled down in their room, and Anthony made a remark about needing to shut the curtains because they were in the Land of Midnight Sun. It was 2:00 a.m. and the sun was just now setting. Here they enjoyed twenty-four-hour daylight in the summer months and twenty-four-hour darkness in the winters. They were exhausted from the trip and fell asleep as soon as their heads hit their pillows. It was eight thirty before they woke up to dress to go and get some breakfast. As they left the room, Anthony noticed an old man leaving his room. Anthony felt that he knew the old man, but he couldn't place him. It immediately brought memories about the note from the waiter in Sanctuary City. Anthony whispered to Amber, "I know this guy, but I don't know from where. Keep on your toes."

They ate breakfast. Both of them were starved. Amber was interested in seeing the sights, especially the volcano, so they went onto the veranda. It was the weirdest sight to view the volcano with lofty clouds swirling about its peak. Every once in a while, the *rjupan* would land and pick up scraps from the guests.[1] They could see occasional drones taking and landing from the air force base. Commercial flights were prohibited now since all transportation was conducted by trains. Looking toward the distant Blafjall Mountains, they could hear the muffled sounds of explosions far in the distance. They were really astounded with the city. Everywhere they looked, the houses were roofed in metal of different colors. There were red, green, orange, blue, and silver roof tops. Of course, they were built exactly same except for the "old city" where the government

---

[1]   Rjupan: A ptarmigan bird common in Iceland.

couldn't dictate the housing. "What a strange place, this Sanctuary City is, Amber. We never hear about rebels from the government radio or television," said Anthony.

"Well, the temperatures here are nice, not hot and steamy like HearthGlen," replied Amber. "And NO slums either."

They returned inside and talked to the same counterperson they met when they arrived at the hotel. "What do you do for entertainment around here?" asked Anthony.

"You won't have to go very far, sir," replied the counterperson. "There isn't any bus service and there are no cabs. Everyone goes to the local taverns. Every neighborhood has its own. Everyone either walks or rides a bicycle. The city isn't very large, and most of it is a restricted area. As I said last night, you've picked a strange place to have a honeymoon."

"I am supposed to meet someone here. Do I have any messages for me?" asked Anthony.

"Let me check. No, sir, no messages." The clerk smiled.

"Okay then, we're going for a walk down into the city," replied Anthony.

"Don't leave without your travel documents, sir," the clerk added.

Amber and Anthony were strolling hand in hand down the street, enjoying the sights of the city. There were few people on the streets as most of the inhabitants were working at this hour. They had been twice stopped by DHS personnel who demanded their travel documents. All was in order, and they were allowed to proceed with warnings about restricted areas in the city. They had strolled through a few streets when they observed another raiding party. Apparently, the FBI and DHS here were busy here too. "Guess HearthGlen has a problem with rebels too," declared Anthony.

"Let's not get involved. We don't need to ask nor answer questions," replied Amber.

They stopped at a café for a snack and cold drinks, and after the waiter took their order, they took a seat outside as the weather was nice. They were engaged in small chat when Anthony nudged Amber's arm. The older gentleman from the hotel was approaching their table.

"Good day," said the man, "I couldn't help but notice you from this morning. I'm staying at the same hotel, the Regency. Mind if I join you?"

"Not at all," responded Anthony. "My name is Tony, and my wife's name is Amber. Please, take a seat."

Anthony sized up their guest—maybe seventy-five-ish, gray-haired, and sporting a modest beard. "And your name is?"

The old man cocked his head to the left and said, "Oh, where have my manners gone? I am called Leo Arthur. Please, call me Leo. I am a businessman by trade."

"I'm an archaeologist by trade myself, and Amber is a professor in linguistics. What type of business of are you in if I may ask?"

"Oh, I trade in futures myself. I don't think that archaeology is a very lucrative business, what with the rebels running around," said Leo.

"Excuse me, but have we met before?" asked Anthony.

Leo scoffed at the idea, saying, "Highly unlikely, I'm afraid. I often get confused for someone else. Have you ever been here before? I've been here myself thousands of times over the years."

The waiter served Anthony and Amber their meal, and Leo ordered some coffee.

Amber smiled to the elderly gentleman and offered, "We are on our honeymoon actually."

"Ah, newlyweds. I was married, but we lost her many years ago. Never did try it again," volunteered Leo. "What languages do you delve into? I have a hard enough time keeping up with this one," laughed Leo.

"I am so sorry for your loss, your wife I mean. Oh, mostly ancient languages. Norse, things like that," said Amber.

Changing the subject, Anthony interceded and said, "So, Leo, you've been here many times. Have you ever seen a volcano act like this one? I'm not a volcanologist, but I've never heard of one act as funny as this one."

Their waiter came by and served Leo his coffee. "Once, but that was many moons ago," chuckled Leo. "Believe me, I used to be a young pup. Yep, it was many moons ago. I—LOOK OUT!" Leo instinctively threw the table on its side and jumped onto Anthony and Amber to shield them. Amber caught a glimpse of a teenager speeding away on a bicycle, who tossed a hand grenade into the café. *BOOM!* It exploded, shattering windows and scattering debris everywhere. It was a terribly loud blast that left their ears ringing. People were screaming everywhere, and the ensuing panic left the customers of the café in shock. Anthony leapt to his feet and ran into the café to render assistance. Luckily, there were just minor injuries, so Anthony ran back to where to his destroyed table used to be.

"You don't want to hang around. The DHS, FBI, and God only knows who else will be swarming this place," Leo yelled. "Run! Get back to the hotel!"

Amber and Anthony scurried back to the hotel, taking a back way to escape detection. Amber was shaken from the ordeal, and they decided to not leave the hotel for the remainder of the day. "How can we trust them now? I'm not sure if I want you involved in this anymore," declared Anthony. "I'm sure it as a random act, but what if it wasn't? What if WE were the target?"

"Tony, we have come too far to back out now. I am not an innocent damsel in distress. I'm a grown woman, and I want to see this to the end," replied Amber. "All I'm saying is that Harald better have some good answers."

"What do you think about us being followed? Someone wants the books besides Harald," asked Anthony. "What is the book about? What's in it?"

"Good questions for Harald to answer," answered Amber.

For two days, both Amber and Anthony didn't leave the room except for meals. They were worried about when they would be contacted by Harald or someone connected to him. They ran into Leo in the hallway, and he stated that he was leaving—going to Fort Hermana to conduct some business there. He wished them well and hoped they enjoyed their stay here in Sanctuary City. Later in the day, the couple heard a light knock at the door. Finally, Harald had showed up. He was admitted into the room. Anthony lit into Harald, asking about the attack at the café and about them being followed and demanding answers.

Harald apologetically answered the questions but denied any involvement with the attack. He conceded that yes, there were others seeking the books and that he would double the security once they left the hotel. Harald said that the rebel groups have increased their attacks. That was why he was delayed. "We need to make haste to get out of the city. Once you leave the hotel, you can't come back here. The book is of utmost importance. You need to find it!"

"What's in the book, anyway?" asked Amber. "What is it so important about it?"

"It tells the future of the world," stated Harald.

"All this . . . this book . . . a fortune teller's book?" asked Anthony incredulously. "A damned book of fortunes, and you spent God-only-knows-how-much money on it?"

"It's not a book about fortune-telling. Anyway, I'm paying for it, so don't belittle me," scolded Harald.

Amber interceded in the conversation and asked, "So, when do we leave?"

"This evening, about six o'clock, so you need to check out of the hotel like normal. I'll need you to meet me at Hog's Head tavern down the street. We'll have to split up. I'll have someone to guide you to our jump-off location. Any questions?" asked Harald.

The couple met as requested, down at Hog's Head tavern. They took a seat in the darkest corner they could find and waited for Harald and his group. They ordered some irish coffee just to fit in with crowd, which was starting to pick up. Not wanting to be noticed, they would occasionally glance about to see if anyone was looking for them. Soon, a scroungy-looking character approached and asked for their travel documents, perused them, and seemed satisfied that all was in order. "Go back in the room over there, one by one. We'll meet you in there," whispered the stranger to Anthony. "Make like you need to use the bathroom."

After a few minutes had elapsed, Anthony made his way to the back room. He was met by two strangers who ordered him to don a cloth bag over his head. "Security," said one of them. It wasn't long before Amber joined them and the same scenario played out. The two guys spun both Amber and Anthony around in an effort to disorient the two, and with the sound of a trapdoor opening, they were led down a flight of stairs. The spinning around occurred twice, and they were hoisted up a vehicle of some kind. For what seemed like an hour, the vehicle sped on what seemed like tracks before coming to a stop. Amber and Anthony were asked if they were all right and then were led away from the vehicle. Soon they were led into a dark room where the cloth bags were removed.

Anthony gasped a breath of fresh air, saying, "Man, I sure am glad to have that bag off my head." He looked around in the room and noticed that Harald was not there. Besides the two guys who led them out to here, there were two additional men present. Anthony observed that the strangers in the room were armed with submachine guns. "I'm Anthony, by the way."

"No names. Security," interrupted one of the men in the room.

"OK, what can I call you then?" asked Anthony.

"Just Dick and Harry, and there is Tom and Larry," answered the guy called Dick.

"Where is Harald?" asked Amber.

"Harald? Never heard of him," replied Larry to Amber's question.

"I'll tell what you need to know. We are to escort you to your destination. We're not a social club, you know," said Larry.

"Well, can I at least ask about where we are going?" said Anthony sarcastically.

"Can you fire a weapon? If we come under attack, can you defend yourself?" asked Harry.

"Yes, I can fire a weapon. I used to own one before Barry and his administration outlawed them. But this is getting us nowhere. Let's try to be civil here. Just tell us where are going?" interjected Amber.

Anthony was stunned by her statement. *I guess she wasn't kidding about not being a damsel in distress,* thought Anthony.

"I have no love for the administration, let's be clear on that. Let's just try to find the damned book," Amber added. The men stopped and just stared at Amber, perhaps feeling foolish because of their boorish attitude.

"All of this is because of a book? What kind of book is it?" asked one of the men in room.

"Oh, just an ancient book. I don't even know if it exists anyway," said Anthony.

"I apologize to you, ma'am. Yes, we will show you the way." Larry brought out a map.

"We will have to either take a boat past the abandoned villages or trek around the mountains to the right." Larry pointed on the map. "Once we get past the old Fort Gate-Pass, it should be a straight shot to here," he said, with a finger pointing on Jarnsmiða. "This will be a dangerous trek. Both ways, we have to keep an eye for drones and stuff. I'd opt for the boat ride myself."

"How long to get there?" asked Anthony.

"Four or five days. But the volcano kinda messes the plans up," replied Larry. "I'd guess about six days. We need to get to Cape Fear Landing, load the supplies, and such."

"We don't have to wear this stupid hood, do we?" asked Amber.

"Nope," was the only answer she received.

Our Journey Begins

The six of them left the room they were staying in, walked to a door, and waited to be sure they weren't detected. It must have been 1:00 am. as the sun was almost overhead. The decrepit building was overrun by weeds, and it was the only building left standing. In this locale, it was usually raining, rather misty, and the tundra afforded little concealment for the six. Amber and Anthony were advised to wear jackets or heavy sweaters as it got real cold fast. "Too bad you didn't bring raincoats. You'll need them once we sail to Ferry Landing," remarked Tom.

"What type of boat is it?" Amber asked.

"Row boat, like a rescue boat. Big too. It was left over from the Great Disaster. We converted it so it runs by cable. Helps when you don't have to man the oars," explained Tom.

The winds were constant here, mostly because of the bay's waters, so Amber snapped her coat closed to ease the biting winds. *Strange land here. We're constantly being bombarded* by *svala,* thought Anthony.[2] *Strange birds. The whirling sounds they make.* The damp ground gave away with each

----
2   Svala: A swallow-like bird common in Iceland.

footstep, making walking difficult. In the background, beyond the Blafjall Mountains, was the volcano, which seemed to be grumbling with anticipation with each step as the group moved closer to it.

"How many drones fly by here?" Anthony quizzed Tom.

"Not many now. Used to be a lot of them. Since the POL tanks have been all but destroyed, they don't have the fuel to send 'em up like they used to," answered Tom.[3] "That's why the trains are always delayed. Due to maintenance—that and our attacks on the trains. I think the war is taking a toll on the administration."

Larry glared at Tom as if to say, "Loose lips sink ships."

Anthony worked his way toward Amber and put his arm over her shoulder, to which she smiled back. "I never dreamt that I would see the outside. Going from the slums to the outside world, I mean. And the attack, well, that was exciting in itself."

"And all because I talked to Harald. I don't regret it all, to be honest with you. I wouldn't have met you," responded Amber.

Anthony blushed slightly at that.

It was about 6:00 a.m. when the group arrived at Cape Fear Landing. They needed to retrieve the boat from a cave on the coastline and put it in the

---

[3]   POL: Petrol, oils, and lubricants. The tanks contain fuels.

water. All the supplies that Harald had promised were in the cave as well. Tom was checking an appliance that detected drones, and nodding his approval, he detected none.

"It will be close to noon when we get to Ferry Landing. Grab some shut-eye in the boat," suggested Larry. "We'll load all the supplies."

"Thanks. We can sure use it," replied Amber. "Let's change into some warmer clothes too."

As they were nearing Ferry Landing, Tom woke up both Amber and Anthony with a jab. "Drone!" he yelled. They were about thirty yards from the shoreline. The two were instructed to lie down in the boat. "Don't move. If it comes this way, wait 'til he fires, then bail out and swim to shore."

"Won't they come looking for us?" asked Anthony.

"Nope. We control the landscape. Besides, no one in his right mind would join the military, especially when they did away with the draft," said Larry. "They fire and then go back to Fort Laekur to rearm. By the time they come back, we'll be long since gone. The FBI, DHS, and TSA—that's all military they have now."

The occupants of the boat were waiting with bated breath, hoping that the drone would fly off. "Good thing is that we were close to shore," added Tom.

But luck was not with them. The shoreline was about twenty feet away when the drone got within striking distance, bucked, and cut loose with a salvo.

The crew of the boat leapt overboard, screaming as they dived as deep as they could into the water. The water was deep enough to prevent shrapnel wounds from the missiles. *Boom!* A shrieking noise was emitted as a second *boom* sounded. The blasts disoriented the submerged crew. Parts of the boat were flying everywhere, followed by splashes as the debris hit the water. The freezing cold from the water shocked them as they surfaced gasping for air. Anthony grabbed Amber by her waist and dog-paddled to shore. They saw the drone do a turn as it returned to Fort Laekur to rearm. Finally, they reached shallow waters and started to wade ashore, exhausted and wet from the frigid waters. "You all right?" Anthony heard someone say.

"Let's find a cave to dry out," Tom declared. "You can't be shy. We got to get out of these wet clothes, and I mean fast! Larry, Dick, get some wood for the fire. The temperatures here will be the death of you if you don't dry our clothes."

The next day, they began their trek to the northwest after they had salvaged the boat and supplies from the water. Some of the supplies, such as the screening equipment and some clothing, couldn't be saved, but they weren't important to the mission.

"Does this happen very often—I mean, the drone attacks?" inquired Anthony.

"Well, yes and no. We can rebuild the boats and such. It is the supplies that are the problem. Like I said yesterday, just lucky we were close to shore," replied Tom.

"We almost never suffer casualties. The drones can pick targets, and they only have two, three rockets to fire off. Then they have to go back to rearm," added Larry. "Because we aren't grouped like in a vehicle or in a building, we do all right for ourselves. It is the artillery fire that does most of the damage to the men. That's why we keep out of range of the artillery batteries. That and the mortar pits around the bases. But it is suicide to mount a ground attack onto the bases."

"Hmm, I guess we were lucky yesterday. How long till we get to Fort Gate-Pass? Do you have a supply depot or something like that?" asked Anthony. "I need warmer clothing. I damned froze my buns off last night."

"Oh, I'd say three days or so. I can check once we get to the fort, but I'm not promising anything. Our soldiers come first," responded Larry.

"But of course." Anthony smiled. "But of course, no question at all."

Anthony rejoined Amber and held her hand tightly while they were lagging behind the escorts. He was really starting to enjoy the excitement and adventure. "Let's start the digs around the castle. Might turn up something there. Then we'll swing up to Jarnsmiða. After all, we decide where and when. To hell with Harald."

"Yep, it's our way or the highway." She started laughing.

"Besides, I need to use the professor skills outside of the classroom. I'd be excited if I actually find something of value."

"You're the boss," Amber said, saluting Anthony.

The group trudged slowly toward the fort, camping several times along the way. They stopped to shoot some rabbits for supper and to rest up. Tom, Larry, Dick, and Harry had loosened up quite a bit, and Anthony deduced from their conversations that the war against the regime was actually going very well. Anthony didn't ask questions about the war effort as he was not a partisan, but he detected in a conversation that the rebel forces have shut down the refinery for POLs. Amber actually loved the wide-open spaces and remarked how beautiful countryside was as she wanted to change the subject to a more pleasant one. She really liked the *svala*, with their dive-bomber tactics and whirring sounds.

Finally, the six of them had arrived at the fort. It was a decrepit place, not very large, and choked with underbrush. Most of the buildings had fallen over the years, and the walls were decaying or had tumbled down. Like most abandoned forts, it was now just a ghost town. Tom yelled out "Heads up!" to declare that they had visitors, to which someone replied "OK." Tom led the group to a building where Tom was asked "What took you so long?" The men manning the fort kept out of sight as they were yelling from the windows of the building.

"Drones, what do you think?" Tom replied rhetorically. "This is the professor and the digging dude, Anthony and Amber."

"I'll be leaving now. Hope you find what you are looking for. The guys here will escort you the rest of the way. If you ever want to join us, we'd be glad to have you," stated Tom. "Oh, almost forgot. The young lady here needs some warmer clothes if you guys can spare 'em"

Amber and Anthony met the group that would escort them to Vokva and Jarnsmiða. The first one they met was John, the leader of the group. He was a balding elderly gentleman with a kind smile. Then there was Steven, a handsome teenager; Fox, a mid-aged man with a scowling face; and Lance, a scholarly gentleman who volunteered to go with them. After the introductions had been made and Amber received a new coat, everyone was briefed on where they were going and what they would be doing. Amber asked if Harald would be joining the group, and the answer was no. He would get updates when needed. It was decided that in the morning, they will be leaving and everyone should get some rest. The journey would take about two days over the mountains surrounding Vokva.

Chapter 3

Vokva and Jarnsmiða

Anthony was walking away from Fort Gate-Pass in a thick, dense fog. He was following Amber, but she couldn't hear Anthony as he yelled as much as he could. He couldn't catch up to her; she was always ahead regardless of how much he ran toward her. She was always appearing in and out of the fog as though she didn't want to be caught. "WAIT UP!" Anthony yelled. It was to no avail as she continued to run. It was snowing—no, not snowing. Rather, it was ashes. Gently snowing ashes as the flakes wafted to the ground. Then came the bolts of lightning. But it wasn't striking down but rather seemed to be building up around him.

Suddenly a huge figure emerged from the darkness calling toward Anthony, "I want it! Give it to me!" The lone stranger then grabbed Amber by her neck and started to strangle her. Then suddenly, *POOF!* Anthony woke up screaming, in a cold sweat, his heart jumping like a jackhammer.

"Are you all right? What happened?" asked Amber as she shook the fog in her sleepy head.

Instead of replying, Anthony leapt out of his cot and ran outside and just stared at Eldfjall. The cone of the volcano was covered with ominous black clouds and occasional bolts of lightning.

"I-it was SO REAL. And the murderous stranger," stammered Anthony. He stared at Amber, feeling foolish, and added, "So real. Do me a favor: try to get a gun from the guys. I feel like I've seen a dark omen. That man . . ."

"What man? What are you talking about? Do you mean Harald?" asked Amber.

"No, the man in my dream—a nightmare, really. He tried to kill you. But he wasn't a man. I mean, yes, he was a man, but huge. I don't know what I mean," responded Anthony. "I'd feel better if you can arm yourself for safety's sake." Anthony could not forget the nightmare. It was because of the books, but what does the volcano have to do with it? And why did the man try to kill Amber?

John, Steven, Fox, and Lance rejoined Amber and Anthony for breakfast. Everyone seemed in great spirits as they looked forward to the trek. The group added a donkey to the caravan for hauling supplies while John issued a revolver to Amber, saying it was a good idea. It was not long before the procession was on its way. Anthony glanced back at the fort and the ever-present backdrop of Eldfjall that slowly diminished with every step they took. He shuddered a bit but quickly recovered by training his sights toward Vokva. They journeyed for about six hours toward the mountains until they detected the frost line, so they decided to stop for lunch. This group was more amicable than the group that had escorted them earlier, and Anthony and Amber found they were likeable fellows.

"How many rebels are with you?" asked Anthony. "I mean, there must be a bunch of 'em."

"Well, I can't say myself, but there is a group just outside of Jarnsmiða. Several hundred, I suppose," responded John. "We have tens of thousands all told, but they are broken up into various factions. And not to mention the supporters in the cities. We will overcome. Eventually we will be victorious."

"What caused you to join the rebels?" queried Amber.

"I, for a lot of reasons. I suppose it was the executions by the regime. A lot of those who have been taken in for questioning and never seen again will never be found. Personally, I'd love to put my hands on Janet and Barry," said Fox. "I guess that we will never find out the number of prisoners who were tortured and executed." Amber looked at Fox, and she detected hate—not just dislike, but true hatred—for Janet and Barry.

The party resumed their trek, and as they neared the mountains, they found *rjupan*, thousands of them. "They are tasty critters," Lance said. "We will set up camp just beyond that pass over there." Lance was pointing to the right and added, "Probably five more hours from here."

"It is beautiful here. Absolutely gorgeous, the scenery here," declared Amber. "No wonder the rebels fled. I'd love to live here. I for one hope to never go back to the city," said Amber to Anthony. "It is so . . . so serene and peaceful here, and the taste of freedom in this vast wilderness . . . ," she said as she wished away.

"Yep, me too. Especially with people disappearing in the cities, all because of the politicians. I had no idea of the executions and people being questioned and never heard from again. People can be so disgusting," said Anthony. "It's because the news media won't tell the truth."

The procession wound up amid the passes and huge boulders. Their breaths were taken away by the scenery. They passed regal geysers spouting toward the skies with the smell of sulfur. They were constantly being bombarded by the *svala*, who seemed to scold them for trespassing on their territories. Amber loved the landscape and constantly made remarks about living free from Barry's administration.

The next day, the group broke camp after resting up. Steven addressed the group and said, "Looks like we are almost to the castle. Be there before four o'clock this afternoon. I've never been there before, but John has. Not much to look at, just old ruins."

"Ah, but I am anxious to take a look. That's what I came for," Anthony replied. "Is it very large?"

John said, "Well, yes and no. It's been abandoned for thousands of years. I guess it's been pretty well picked over by the scavengers. Still, some old statues around to look at though if you're interested."

Off in the distance, they could hear the muffled blasts from drones striking some targets. They were too distant, so John disregarded the strikes. "You don't have to worry about the drones. They don't target anything around here. Mostly, they just stay near Fort Gate-Pass and the strongholds up toward Jarnsmiða and Fort Hermana. They take off and land from Fort Hermana, but between the airports getting bombed all the time and the ones that we shoot down, those drones are a nuisance rather than a threat."

It wasn't long before they had reached Vokva. John decided to pitch camp, so they went about setting up the tents and unloading the supply mule. Anthony and Amber wandered closer to the ancient fortress to see it for themselves. It appeared to have been carved out of the mountain, and the handiwork was painstakingly done well. There were remnants of a moat, a broken drawbridge, and a huge statue of a dwarf long since broken by earthquakes and age. It was an awesome sight to see, and it fueled their eagerness to visit in the morning. Both of them were awestruck at having seen the citadel. Anthony turned to Amber and asked, "Did you really mean it when you said you'd like to live here?"

"Tony, I really meant it. There's nothing I would love more. The freedom, the fresh air, the scenery. But mostly, I want to spend time with you," responded Amber, and with that, she kissed Anthony.

The Citadel

It was a superb day, with little wind, as Anthony stood outside of the tent. He was scrutinizing from afar the dwarven statue with its lifeless stony eyes, as if it was staring back at Anthony. It was 6:00 a.m., and the group would soon be up and about. "I should start on the diary. Document findings and such," said Anthony to himself.

> 30 Jun 2014
>
> Today starts the first day looking for artifacts. We scouted around the moat area, viewed the dwarven statues high atop the walls, but we need to find a way to get over the moat as the drawbridge has collapsed. 0600

Amber stirred inside the tent. She was putting on her hiking boots. She couldn't wait to get up and examine the statues. She greeted Anthony with a "Mornin'" as she exited the tent. "Should we wait for the others to get up, or just 'dig in'?" She laughed.

Anthony smiled and said, "Let's go then."

When they reached the edge of the moat, they wondered how they could traverse it without grappling. Below them was the, broken drawbridge, the wooden planks long since disappeared over the ages. They brought ropes with them, but those were not enough to span the crevasse. They decided to lower themselves to the moat bottom, hoping to find a grating. Most likely, they would find where the source of the long-dried-up stream of water came from. The bottom was filled with boulders and remnants of parts of the walls and pieces of the arms from the statues overhead. Finally they found a grate that granted them access to the citadel itself. It was a tight squeeze, but they managed to get through it. It was dark inside, but at the end of the tunnel, they found a beam of light leading to the egress. Exiting the tunnel, they were greeted by the cawing of ravens that fled from the interlopers.

It was a wonderful sight, with the long cobblestone corridor leading into the castle. They could almost picture in their minds how regal and picturesque it must have been. If only the lone statue perched above the castle entrance could speak—the wondrous tales it must know. It was at least thirty feet tall and missing an arm, but the hammer in its hand told of power, strength, and honor. The workmanship of the sculptor was exquisite, the statue bearing full plate armor. "This is what I've always wanted to behold," said Anthony with awe in his voice.

"Yes, yes, I couldn't agree more," Amber replied. "And look over there—the Norse writing under the statue. 'King Magnus tending his mighty forge.'"

Anthony tried to picture the lofty citadel as it must have been many centuries ago. It was almost magical, with King Magnus surrounded with his knights. Amber and Anthony wandered the fortress. They saw the reception hall, the dining hall, the quarters for the soldiers, and the castle marketplace, and they lost time because of it. "Well, Amber, I need to jot down some notes in the diary. Can you find your way back to the camp?" asked Anthony.

"Of course, my dear. Not a problem. At least, I found the way into the castle." Amber beamed.

After Amber left and he began to inscribe into his diary, Anthony was caught up in a daydream. He was a knight, one of the regal cavaliers serving the king. All around his mounted steed were the adoring peasants, chanting, as he and his fellow knights assembled in the castle grounds as they prepared to depart for battle. He was adorned in his shiny plate armor with a tabard bearing the hammer of Thor. "One for all, all for one! Victory is near! Strike down the enemies of the monarchy!" he screamed.

All of a sudden, a whispery gust of wind blew a page from his diary, which ended his daydream. He chased the paper across the courtyard, letting the scrap of the paper descend against the leg of a dwarven statue. "Traikon," whispered the wind as it disappeared. It wasn't exactly a spoken word but a feeling. "Where do I know that name from? I can't remember, but where?" asked Anthony to himself. Then he caught a glimpse of something odd, perhaps out of place. He knelt down and blew dirt and dust from a corner of the statue's pedestal. "Holy smoke, I think I found something! Amber over—" Anthony cut his sentence short; she was already gone. Anthony carefully marked the location of the find and headed back to camp.

As Anthony neared the camp, he yelled out, "Amber! Amber, I found something! Come quickly!" as he ran to the group at the campsite.

"Already? What have you found?" requested Amber. "You're a fast worker!"

He was all out of breath as he knelt to gasp some air. "I . . . I need you . . . to help rope the area off," panted Anthony.

After gaining his composure, Anthony said, "Sure lucky, I am," as he paused for a moment. "A gust of wind blew a page from the journal, and the paper landed right on it. At first I didn't notice it when I picked up the page, but then I looked a second time, and I noticed that the pedestal for the statue—it was odd. Bring me some twine and my toolkit so we can figure out what it is."

"Well, luck is a big part when digging. The city of Troy was found because of luck," asserted Amber as she was getting excited about the find.

John and Steven volunteered to join the dig, and Lance and Fox decided to stay behind as Lance was the cook for the group and Fox was to be the gofer for the group.

It wasn't long before Anthony was directing the dig team. They needed to mark the boundaries for the site, isolate the pedestal around the statue, and blow the ground in the marked spot. For hours, the four of them toiled on their hands and knees, being careful of not digging too fast or too deep. Every ounce of the excavated area had to be checked as they really had no idea what they were looking for. Anthony worked at the base of the pedestal, gently scraping the soil, blowing, and then scraping again. It was painstaking work. Everyone had to take breaks because it was a killer on their knees and backs. Fox brought lunch, then dinner, and finally a late snack for the group. Finally, they called it a night due to the lateness of the day. When they stood back and surveyed the dig site, they noticed that they had barely scratched the surface.

"I hope this doesn't take an eternity," remarked Anthony.

1 July 2014

We marked the site and started the dig. Hopefully, we can make some real progress tomorrow. I can almost see

what appears to be a panel, but it could
be an etching of some kind. 0020

Anthony did not sleep very well that night. He had
visions of Eldfjall, which was always under the cover of
ominous dark clouds. And then was something about
the secretive creature called Traikon. He was always
beckoning toward him, kind of like he was wanting
something; but to what end? And what of Mortikon?
What is he—a creature or some kind of god?

15 July 2014:

We have excavated some steps behind
the statue. There is definitely a panel of
some kind, but how far do we have to dig
to get to the bottom? Amber said that
the runes seem to say *Mortikon*, but is it
a god or a king? 2200

Everyone was holding their breath to see if the
cross was a kind of key. Perhaps what lay behind
the panel would be something of value. As Anthony
pushed the cross into the slot, a faint clicking sound
came from the opening. Anthony immediately realized
that it was indeed a key, as a smirk came upon his
face. The panel groaned a bit as it hadn't been opened
for a millennium, but slowly, the panel gave in.

"What's in there?" asked John as his anticipation
grew. "Let us take a look, wouldya?"

Amber gasped. She could see a case made of gold. Steven whistled, astounded because it was indeed a valuable artifact. The gold case spoke of money.

Anthony retrieved the case as carefully and delicately as he could. He was savoring the moment, not wasting any of it.

"Well? Open it!" demanded Amber.

As soon as the case was opened, the ground trembled slightly. Everyone felt it, leaving them with a feeling of discomfort.

Anthony carefully lifted the case, and inside was a replica of the cross! He retrieved the one that had been used to open the panel and compared the two of them. The only difference between them was the inscription, "Mortikon." He closed the golden coffin after replacing the newly found artifact. "Well, I guess that Harald should be told of the find."

2 August 2014

We have completed the excavation, which revealed a panel with a design etched to the right. It seems like it was made exactly like the cross that had been given to me by Harald. 1015

With that, the group returned to their campsite to examine the new discovery. John left to go back to Fort Gate-Pass to let Harald know of the finding. He would be gone about five days, so they decided to explore more of Vokva. In Vokva, they found several odds and ends and some trinkets, but nothing close to the cross. There were several inscriptions throughout the citadel bearing *Mortikon*, but the group did not have enough information about what or who this Mortikon could be. Is this Mortikon a god? The only thing they could come up with was the suspicion that the nightmares were connected—but how and why?

Finally, the days of waiting and doing nothing except hanging around the camp came to an end.

The Forge

John didn't return to the campsite. Rather, three new strangers showed up, all of them unknown to Anthony and Amber. Apparently Steven, Lance, and Fox had been reassigned to other duties, so both and Amber and Anthony met the new members. It was Trey, Carl, and a man called Cheese. *A suspicious group,* thought Amber.

Trey brought news from Harald that they needed to disband the campsite and proceed to Jarnsmiða. The three new members were not very gregarious and mostly spoke only between themselves in hushed tones. Like the old groups, these were armed with rifles and were very intimidating to be around. When the man called Cheese was asked about his name, he only replied, "Nickname."

"The mission will only be to retrieve the book," said Carl with a snarl. "That is the ONLY responsibility you will have. You got it?"

Unlike the other parties, this one did not help with dismantling the campsite. Between the groaning and complaints within the new party, both Amber and Anthony were left with a feeling of unease. When asked if Harald would join the group, Trey only responded, "Perhaps."

Anthony asked how long they would be on the road, and Cheese replied, "Two days or so. Once we hit the foothills, we will turn to the west. The forge will be wedged between two hills. Gotta keep a sharp eye out for bandits. They are a different faction of rebels."

It started raining—not a downpour but a mist—as the four of them neared the Blafjall Mountains. The eternally shrouded peaks of Eldfjall were always present, sending booms through the air as though the streaks of lightning were beckoning the group, warning the group off. It seemed it was sending a message: Stay Away. The closer the gang encroached Jarnsmiða's territory, the more the activity around Eldfjall increased. Both Amber and Anthony seemed to sense an evil presence from within the volcano. Plodding along, the party remained silent, walking immersed in their own thoughts. Anthony thought it was a good thing that he kept the derringer. Occasionally, the hair on Anthony's neck would seem to stand up as if to warn him of danger, but when he looked, he couldn't detect anything. It only increased his awareness of the things around him.

For two days, the group urged toward their destination until, finally, the trek was over. Lying before them was the ancient citadel Jarnsmiða. It wasn't much to look at—scruffy vines all over the paths, overgrown with weeds and such. Some of the vines were as thick as Anthony's arm, and the odors gave off a stench, a horrible smell. As they neared the vines, they found why the smell was present: the vines were carnivorous, and everything they touched, the vines would wrap around as a feast. Any animals that were unfortunate enough to venture close were doomed. There was a lack of bird life in the vicinity. The silence was deafening. In front, the forge was surrounded by crumbly walls perhaps thirty feet tall and set with a dilapidated iron gate, long silent through the ages. It took almost four hours taking machetes against the creepy vines, but they finally made their way through them. After four hours of toil, the group was exhausted, and they fell to the ground, grateful for the rest.

It was 5:00 p.m., and Anthony decided to pitch camp inside the compound to which Carl snapped back and said, "I'll tell you when and what to do."

An exhausted Amber flew into a rage and retorted, "You can shove your orders up your arse! You've not spoken a civil word with us, and you have the gall to order US around! Without us, your Harald buddy will be dead in the water, so shove it!"

Carl hesitated, seemingly getting ready to raise his weapon, decided against it, and replied, "Have it your way, bitty. But don't think for one moment that you are in charge. WE are." Carl was furious and his eyes shot hatred at her. It was a typical Mexican standoff, so Anthony grabbed her arm and led her away.

Whispering to Amber, Anthony said, "I don't care much for our crew, but let's try to find this damned book. I'm afraid one of them will shoot us in the back. Keep an eye out for them. They are as suspicious of us as we are of them, so watch your back, hon. Man, do I have some harsh words for Harald when he shows up!"

Anthony and Amber retired for the night, but not before they noticed that Cheese was posted as a sentry. Whether it was because he was posted for their safety or to insure that he could prevent them from leaving without the book was the question. It was mid-August. The sunset was at midnight, with sunrise at four thirty, which was normal for this time of the year. What weren't normal though were the nightmares that occurred more often—always with the same theme, centered on Traikon and Mortikon. Eldfjall was churning as if it had a stomachache and belched out with minor quakes. From their roiling black masses above the volcano, the clouds emitted bolts of thunderous lightning that escaped into the night air. Anthony stirred in his sleep, roused by the nightmare. It was 6:00 a.m., so he decided to dress himself and left the tent. As expected, Cheese was still there, saying nothing but glaring at Anthony. He walked to the campfire and grabbed a cup of coffee, swished it down, and refilled the cup for Amber. She was still asleep, so he left the cup next to her cot, and he left his tent to survey the forge. *As soon as he gets his damned book, then we're outta here,* thought Anthony. *I wonder if they will even help us to get back to HearthGlen.*

Anthony walked around the compound, which had several broken-down structures in it. He wondered what the buildings were used for in their heyday when they were still functional. Perhaps no one would ever know. Off to the side of the compound was a building. Its roof and a part of its wall had collapsed. Anthony surmised that they were victims of earthquakes. The main forge facility, however, was hewn from the cliffs. It had obviously been made by many thousands of dwarfs whittling the stone façade. He noticed an odd statue, something like an out-of-place figurine, of a sphinx. Half human and half ox, it must have been of religious significance to the creators of the forge. As he scrutinized the statue, he felt tremors in the ground. "Best if I can warn the others to look out for falling rocks," Anthony said to himself. He walked through the gate of the forge just so he could get a feel of how big it was inside. The innermost hall was littered with boulders and fallen walls and two, perhaps three, rooms, all with massive roofs. He completed his cursory walk-through and returned to the camp.

Anthony entered the tent that he and Amber were using where he found her enjoying the coffee. Whispering, he asked, "Do you still have the pistol?

I don't like the situation here. Is it me, or do you sense a dreadful evil force here?"

In hushed tones, Amber agreed with him. "Yep. And it's loaded too. I think we are prisoners of the three clowns, and I don't doubt at all that we'll wind up getting killed. I feel a sense of dread about this place, but not like you. Maybe it's my imagination, but ever since we left Fort Gate-Pass, you've been plagued worse by those nightmares. I for one will not miss this place once we leave."

They left the tent together and were accosted by Trey. "It will be September soon, which means snow. Can you pick up the pace a bit? I don't know where you come from, but here, we can get tons of snow."

"Sure thing, boss," replied Anthony. The snow lines in the mountains were slowly but surely creeping down, and the group didn't have the cold-weather gear required to spend more time before they would be forced to leave.

"We're heading into the forge now, if you are interested."

Anthony and Amber gathered up their equipment and headed out.

Amber was reading the Norse runes as they passed through main entrance. *Þórs hamar eldstæði* it said. She deciphered the symbols as "Thor's Hammer-Forge."

"Oh, by the way, I need to warn you. I felt some tremors earlier when I was here," advised Anthony.

The two of them explored the empty rooms, crisscrossing between the fallen boulders. One of the rooms had apparently been used as a crypt for fallen soldiers. They were empty, as if scavengers had defiled the sacred grounds. The third door led downward, but it was too dark to see very far. Amber suggested they should map out the areas they explored in case the dig site ended up being very large. Anthony agreed with her and needed to gather some torches, and he advised her not to enter for safety reasons while he was away. He returned with helmeted lights and said that the battery lights would suffice.

It was dank and murky as soon as they passed through the door. Everything was covered in dust—either from the falling debris because of the numerous earthquakes or from the accumulation from the centuries of grime. The ceiling was covered with bats hanging down, and the floor was crawling with roaches and centipedes. Spiderwebs were abundant there as they had to brush them aside. Amber had to look up the inscriptions of the runic symbols, and she said, "*Böðull gnagadyr*. Rat control. Guess they had rat problems back then." She laughed. "I guess that is the way toward rat control."

"Too bad three of them escaped and are in our campsite," laughed Anthony. "What lies ahead through this door?" asked Anthony. "We'll check this room first and then descend the stairs. Be careful, the stair steps may give way."

"Hmm, looks like—can't quite read it. It is so old. Got it. It means *supplies*," replied Amber.

After checking the supply room and finding there were three more doors in there, Anthony decided that he needed to map the rooms as they didn't want to get lost. In the supply room was a line of ancient torches. "We'll just make the translations and move to the next one. I'll bet we will find the books in the library, if we can ever find it," she decided.

Four hours had elapsed, and they were forced to retreat due to lack of batteries for the headlights. The two of them had reached the campsite, and while stowing their notes and getting fresh batteries, they asked for some help exploring the caverns. Trey volunteered, saying he didn't have anything important to do, and after lunch, the three of them returned to the forge. They surveyed three floors of the forge and finally had to stop due to a huge crevasse in the floor. It was about thirty-five feet wide, and by dropping stones into to the gaping hole, Anthony judged it to be about five hundred feet deep. There seemed to be another door in the distance, but how do they get there?

"We need to turn around. This cavern is nothing but a maze of endless doors. Besides, we don't have enough batteries to search endlessly. This place is nothing but mazes. It may take a bit before we find the library. We can try some of the torches we found in the supply room if they still work," advised Anthony.

It was now September 12, and the first snows were threatening. The group had almost finished mapping the forge, and they recovered plenty of artifacts but no books. Amber and Anthony were about to give up unless they could find a way past the chasm. They also found humongous spiderwebs, with strands almost as thick as Anthony's wrist. The spiders must have been as large as a modern-day tank. But they needed to know how to span the fissure in the forge. The library had to lie beyond that door. The group didn't have enough rope to cross the gaping hole, and everyone was flummoxed by figuring out how to do it. Time was not on the side of the group. Another two weeks and they would have to abandon the quest.

Anthony had another nightmare in the middle of the night, again centered on Traikon and Mortikon. Only this time, dwarfs and goblins were in it, RIDING spiders! Traikon, a shadowy figure, beckoned toward Anthony, but it was not Anthony he wanted. He was calling out for a guy named Agnar—now Stefan—and then a figure called Rober! But he was speaking to Anthony, not Agnar, Stefan, or Rober. Mortikon seemed to be smiling as he reached out for a book. As always, the volcano was in the background. Suddenly, Anthony bolted out of his nightmare, sat up in the cot, and yelled, "GOT IT!"

He ran to the cot on which Amber slept and shook her awake. "I got it! I know how to reach the door!" Anthony's nightmare gave them the solution to the chasm!

Book of Knowledge

Anthony and Amber, along with Trey, were in the room where they had found the huge spiderwebs. Armed with machetes, they were whacking away at the biggest web strands that they needed. "Here were the ropes we needed, just under our noses," said Anthony gleefully. "We can use these to make our own ropes." They busily set about to braid the web strands with the existing rope, and soon, they had enough rope to span the hole. It wasn't long before the trio began to grapple, hand over hand, with the rope. For just over an hour it took, but they eventually made it to solid ground with the door just before them. Finally, they were about to find out what lay beyond the last door. They reequipped themselves and set off for their last leg of the quest. Beyond the door was a stone wall and a set of steps into the darkness below. A bunch of Norse symbols were there, with arrows leading to the right and left. "*Eldstæði. Forge,*" Amber translated and pointed down the steps. "*Eldhús. Kitchen,*" she said as she pointed to the right. "I'd love to find a fully functionally kitchen right now." Amber laughed.

"I wonder how many floors to reach the bottom?" said Anthony with no one in mind.

They traversed the steps down, watching for weak steps. Many steps gave away under their weight as the countless earthquakes had taken their toll on them. At the bottom were three more doors, one to the left that Amber interpreted as "*Fanga klefa*. Dungeon." The middle door went toward the main forge, and to the right, the door had the inscription . . . "*Safn*. Library! We found it!" Amber said, feeling elated as the quest would soon be over.

Anthony instructed Trey to go back and let everyone know that they had located it, but before he left, Trey admonished the other two to do nothing until he came back. *Yeah, right,* thought Anthony. *I bet you would like that.*

After Trey left, Anthony warned Amber to not turn her back toward them when they got back. "Keep your pistol ready. I don't trust any of them." Anthony entered the library with Amber in tow. There were thousands of books, most of them too fragile to touch lest they turn to dust. But which book? Or books? How would he know which one or ones? This was a quandary; perhaps Harald would have to find it.

Amber tried to blow the dust off from one book and the book vanished into dust. "These would be priceless if you could preserve them, literally worth a king's ransom," she breathed.

Row after row they traversed the books, when suddenly a humming sound, like a cell phone left on mute receiving something, was heard. They couldn't locate where the sound was coming from. Then Anthony detected a low hum coming from his knapsack—not only from the cross but ALSO from the gold case containing the second cross. He grabbed the two crosses from the knapsack and immediately saw a shimmery blue glow emitting from the two crosses, the original one and the gold-encased one. He opened the gold case and picked it up, and suddenly, the two crosses became one! As if magic, the two crosses merged together, and immediately, they heard a low growl, like a scraping noise, as a panel began to open. Beyond the secret door, the room began to glow a bluish tint, enveloping both of them with the color. Inside, on a table, were three books—*The Books of Knowledge!* Both stood agog, unable to speak, their totally rapt bodies could do nothing except stare.

Taken aback, Anthony and Amber did not notice that suddenly behind them Harald and Lillian. They were surprised when Harald said, "At last! My whole life I have searched for these books. I KNEW from the start that you were the one—" The report sounded from a pistol from behind as he slumped to the floor. Standing over the body was Lillian, with a smoking gun in her hand.

In a cold, calculated voice Lillian said, "Put the books in the knapsack and throw it to me. Careful there." She waved the pistol menacingly toward Amber and Anthony.

"W-Why did you kill Harald? I thought you were partners?" asked Amber.

"You worm, I did it for power, money. Mortikon will reward me handsomely, perhaps let me rule this world," threatened Lillian. She aimed at Amber and added, "One false move, and you are dead," she warned Amber. "Throw your pistol to me. Carefully, butt first." Amber complied with the command, and the pistol clanked as it hit the ground. "I'm not armed," Amber declared.

"Mortikon? Who is this Mortikon character?" demanded Anthony. "I've never heard of the Mortikon."

Lillian interrupted him and said, "Enough of this! Throw the bag to me, NOW!"

Anthony was stalling for time. He asked, "And your henchmen, Carl, Trey, and Cheese, are they working for you?"

"Of course, you dolt. Throw the bag to me NOW!" said Lillian.

With that, he threw the bag at Lillian with enough power to interrupt her concentration. With that, Anthony jarringly aimed and fired his derringer at the same moment Lillian cut loose with a shot from her pistol. She fell to the floor, and Anthony ran forward and kicked her pistol away from her. He retrieved the knapsack, and when he turned, he saw Amber on the floor. He ran to Amber crying, "Nooooo." Lillian's shot had hit Amber in the chest. With that, the Eldfjall launched a massive earthquake, as if in a fit of rage.

There was no escaping now as the walls began to crumble. With no option open, Anthony dragged Amber inside the secret room, where he noticed a semitransparent orb in the corner. "Do or die," said Anthony as he pulled Amber and knapsack into the portal.

KAFLI:

EPISODE TWO

Once upon a time, we used to believe in magic and wondrous things. There was a time when everyone believed in Santa Claus and the Easter Bunny and fairies. It was a wonderful thing to have beliefs, whether or not they brought hope and love and belief in change for mankind. Yes, it was indeed magical, but sometimes, some things were not as they seemed. There were always bogeymen around: the ogres, the trolls, and evil witches and warlocks. But a change was about to overcome the world. For now, the world has entered an era of murkiness, where evil overcomes the days and nights and the innocence of children. Mortikon has risen again, and with his powers of deception, his rage, and his lust of power, he has launched a new campaign of evil upon the world. He will not rest until *The Book of Knowledge* is in his possession. He has assembled a vast army in the north that is just waiting for the command: "TO WAR."

Chapter 4

Once Upon a Time

Prince Maura was kneeling on one knee before his master, Lord Mortikon, as they discussed the attempt to gain possession of *The Book of Knowledge*. Prince Maura was a handsome, well-dressed, and extremely intelligent man perhaps of fifty years of age. His long blond hair attracted more observers of him, which fit with his person very well. Lord Mortikon, or rather his hologram, was giving instructions to Prince Maura. After Mortikon had been banished from the world, he could only communicate through such means. For you see, Mortikon was a *leiche*, one of the undead, ever since an elven warrior named Agnar had slain him in combat by using the Great Sword, Mjölnir, which transformed him into a *leiche*. He was a frightful warrior, dressed fully in shiny black plate armor, armed with a broadsword, and was both appalling as well as appealing to look upon. His presence was both charismatic and evil at the same time, but make no mistake about it: he was cold, harsh, and evil.

"I want the book, and I don't care how you do it, but bring the book to me," said Mortikon with a voice of authority. "I want the lineage of Agnar silenced. Bring me the head of Anthony."

"But *Anthony* isn't an elven name," replied Prince Maura.

"You can call him any name you wish, but he is here. Among you here and now, I can feel his presence. Seek him out, bring me the book and his head!" screamed Mortikon. "I want the curse from Agnar and his descendants lifted from me!"

"Yes, my lord," replied Maura. "Your wish is my command."

Prince Maura took leave of Mortikon and gathered his minions together. "I want your best scryers on this job," demanded Prince Maura from General Snagtann.

General Snagtann, a muscular green-skinned orc with massive fangs protruding from his lower jaw, saluted the prince. "I'll have our spies in the south on it right away, sire," he replied to the prince. "I will increase the number of wraith riders along the borders too."

Anthony fell into the portal with the wounded Amber as he clutched the knapsack that contained the book. What he found beyond the portal stunned him beyond words. He was a confronted by a long-haired, bearded old man wearing *robes*—not bath robes, but robes of a wizard or mage. Standing next to the old man was a little boy, in a similar attire. The little boy couldn't be more than three and half feet in height. The newcomers were in a room set up like a chemistry student´s lab. But this wasn't a student's lab. The little boy was working on potions of some type.

Anthony was beside himself, weeping as Amber was dying. "H-help," cried Anthony. "S-she is dying. Please, help me."

The old man snapped a finger toward the little boy as a signal to seek help. The old man helped carry Amber onto a table to examine the wound. He uttered a *tsk* while he inspected the injury. Amber was pale and cold. It was obvious she was dying, and her eyes weren't responding.

"Can't you do something?" asked Anthony frantically.

Then the old man started chanting as he held his hands over the wounded area.

"D-Do something, please!" pleaded Anthony. "Don't you speak English? She is dying!"

Then assistance arrived—in the form of the little boy and a dwarf! The dwarf, attired in leather armor, stood at the head of the table and started chanting. The little boy was busy mixing a red-colored potion, a vile-looking potion, and administrated the medicine.

"Is that all you can do? Chant? She is dying for christ's sake!" Anthony admonished the helpers.

Suddenly the chanting stopped, and right before his own eyes, Anthony saw that the wound was healing! Amber gasped, and Anthony could see color rushing back into her once-pallid skin.

"She be healed in a few minutes," declared the old man. "What manner of beast be ye? And thine court jester? What manner of costume be ye dressed? I know not how ye came before me."

Stunned by their mannerisms and style of speech, Anthony was bewildered, and stammered, "B-but, I'm human, not a beast. A-and I can ask you the same questions. Where am I? Who are you?"

Apparently the dwarf, little boy, and old man was just as perplexed as Anthony. Anthony was startled as Amber suddenly sat up. "Who—? How—? Where are we?" she asked.

Anthony shook his head, bunched his shoulders up, and said nothing. He grinned widely and examined the wound. There was no wound! "Am I dreaming? I saw you at near death. Look, I still have your blood on my clothes. Can anyone explain any of this?"

"Nay, 'tis no dream. Skuli be me name, me trade be priest. Why ye be here, in HearthGlen? And what, perchance, be thy name?" inquired Skuli to Anthony.

"Anthony is my name, and this here is Amber. Why are we here? I remember we were in Jarnsmiða, in the library. Two people were killed there and then an earthquake hit."

"Jarnsmiða? Me family be from Vokva. Me name be Thor. Me trade be paladin," explained the dwarf, Thor.

"And me be Hafsteinn. Me trade be Mage," piped up the boy, Hafsteinn.

"I must be dreaming. A paladin, a mage, and a priest. How can this be? And your clothes. Robes and *armor*? What year is this?" asked Anthony.

Amber looked around, and her astonishment grew for on the walls were runic symbols! "Yes, exactly what year is this?"

"Why 'tis the year of Highness King Aegir, of course," answered Hafsteinn with a puzzled look on his face.

Amber was as puzzled as Anthony, as the rule of King Aegir meant nothing to them. "Well, little boy, can you—"

"Little boy? *Little boy!* I be older than ye. I am no apprentice, so kindly hold yer tongue," interrupted Hafsteinn briskly before Amber could finish speaking.

Amber was embarrassed and apologized profusely toward Hafsteinn, and she asked, "If Thor is a dwarf and Skuli is a human, then what are you?"

"Why, I be a gnome, can ye not see with yer own eyes?" answered Hafsteinn.

"Huh. Humans, dwarfs, gnomes. This is too much to comprehend," said Anthony. "What other races live here? Please don't muddle my mind with ogres and trolls."

"Eh? What ya mean? We have elves, ogres, trolls, and orcs," responded Thor.

"Th-this is like a fairy tale to me," stammered Anthony. "Please wake me up. I need some time to comprehend all this."

All that Amber could do was remain sitting on the table and stare with her dropped jaws, unable to say anything.

After the initial shock and confusion wore off, the myriad of questions began. Both the newcomers and their hosts showering each other with questions. The newcomers interrogated their hosts with the typical *hows*, *whats*, *wheres*, and *whos*, and answering, their hosts had questions of their own. Eventually, Hafsteinn was instructed by Skuli to get their guests some suitable clothing from downstairs. Anthony had totally forgotten about the knapsack and the contents. "Oh, yeah, we found some old books in the library just before the earthquake. Some type of *Book of Knowledge*," said Anthony as he reached in to retrieve the contents.

"*DON'T TOUCH THEM!*" screamed Skuli. "By the gods, if they are the book, then they be sacred. Only Traikon, the guardian, may touch them. Do not open the knapsack! My worst fears be upon us. Mortikon will unleash his evil upon us. I must summon one for advice in this grave event."

"Who are Traikon and this Mortikon? Everyone talks about this Traikon and Mortikon," asked Anthony. "I found this in Vokva." Anthony produced the amulet key and showed it to them.

Skuli stood back a step refusing to let his hands touch the amulet. "By the gods, 'tis the Arkaain! As for Mortikon, why, Mortikon is the leader of the evil forces of the world, of course," replied Skuli. "Traikon is the savior of the little peoples."

"The little peoples?" asked Anthony with a perplexed face.

Skuli considered for a moment and replied, "The gnomes, dwarfs, elves, and goblins."

Soon Hafsteinn returned with clothes for Amber and Anthony—simple garb used by peasants. After changing clothes, Thor invited the two atop the wizards' tower to view HearthGlen.

Anthony just stared. He couldn't believe what he was looking at. Flying overhead were huge eagles being piloted by people! The airlifted people were using eagles for transportation. And the ministry buildings were gone—in their place was a castle! A actual castle, with moats and knights scurrying everywhere!

Amber just stood in awe. The world as she knew it had been turned upside down. From being at death's doorstep to her miraculous healing to the existence of the magical creatures in the forms of dwarfs, gnomes, and elves. She couldn't comprehend it all. "Tony, please tell me I'm dreaming."

Anthony turned his thoughts toward the knapsack. If everything was real, then the book must be real too. And if it was real, just the thought of possessing the *Book of Knowledge* was unthinkable.

The three of them went back into the wizards' tower, and before them was a new stranger, who was looking at the knapsack. He was a magnificent specimen to behold, perhaps fifty-five years of age, with golden hair, a long beard, and with a sparkle in his eyes. He neared them with an extended hand, and he said, "Ah, our unexpected guests, I see. I am Oskar the White. I am at your command."

"Good to meet you. I am Anthony, and this is Amber," answered Anthony.

"The prophets of old have foretold your arrival here. I'm almost certain that before our eyes are the tomes of the book. Take a seat, for what I have to tell you will perhaps shock you," offered Oskar. Both Amber and Anthony accepted their seats as Oskar continued. "You two will be hunted, not only by Mortikon, but by humans as well. What you have in your possession is the most important and deadliest weapon in the universe: knowledge. The beginning to the end of the cosmos, whole worlds both founded and yet to be discovered are contained within. I know of you. I have always known of you, Anthony Ragnarsson. The quest before you is fraught with danger. Your quest is simple: destroy the book. Should Mortikon gain the book, all will be lost, and the world will be plunged into darkness and evil."

"And how do I destroy it? Not by burning I presume," asked Anthony.

"We shall explain it all later, as secrecy is important. We shall travel to the elven realm, Helgilands, to meet with your ancestors," explained Oskar.

"W-what? I-I'm an *ELF?*" stuttered Anthony.

"Oh, you shall learn much about yourself within the weeks to come," replied Oskar the White.

Revelations

Both Amber and Anthony were shocked when Oskar disclosed that Anthony was indeed an elf. All Anthony could do was to shake his head in disbelief. The entire chain of events for the day was mind-numbing. Anthony wanted to hear more, but Oskar declined to answer any more questions for the day, saying that they needed to get some rest and sort out their entire lives. "Tomorrow, my child, in the morrow. Have you not heard enough for one day?" asked Oskar.

Anthony and Amber awoke in a confused state of mind. They were still clad in peasants' clothes; they were still in a room with cradles padded with straw. And they were starving! They were excited about the new surroundings and their hosts. They were loaded with questions they were eager to find answers to. They ran up the stairs, hoping to quench their knowledge of this newfound land. Everything was so new to them; they were like children longing to slake their excitement. They found Oskar, Skuli, and Hafsteinn sitting at the table enjoying breakfast in the next room.

"Greetings, my new friends," said Amber. "What is for breakfast? I'm starved."

"Ah, our guests have arrived," declared Oskar. "Just some flaxen bread, some cheese, and skyr, help yourselves to our bounty."[4]

The cheese had a pungent smell, and the bread was excellent. They had never tasted bread so good, and the cheese was marvelous.

"How do I eat skyr?" asked Anthony. "We have never tried it in our time."

"Just put some sugar and blueberries and mix it with milk," chuckled Oskar.

The skyr looked like thick mass and had a gooey texture, and Amber sniffed it before she tried it. "Say, this is wonderful," declared Amber as she had tried a spoonful.

During breakfast, both Amber and Anthony were peppering their new hosts with new questions. "How did you take me from the verge of death to . . . well, back to normal health? And within minutes, I may add," quizzed Amber of her hosts.

"'Tis magic, of course. Me training be's in the Priest Guild. Thor can heal as well, but not as well as me. Thor gotta his training in the Paladin Guild. Hafsteinn here, be's in the Mage Guild, makes good potions with his alchemy skills," answered Skuli.

Anthony interceded with "We have elixirs called medicines in our time. But the healing—now that is new to me."

---

4   Skyr: A concoction like yogurt—very delicious—which is eaten in milk and is popular in Iceland.

"Alas, for the healing touch is a dying art. Now only priests and paladins are taught," replied Skuli sadly.

The entire group was engrossed in conversation. The guests were as full of questions as the hosts were too. It wasn't long before the conversation turned to exactly what the book was and how they were intending to destroy it. "As I said yesterday, all of your questions will be answered in due time," said Oskar. "But we need to get you out of HearthGlen for your lives will be forfeit if you don't leave. The spies of Mortikon will be here soon, if not already here. We need some weapons. Daggers and swords, bows as well. I fear the darkness will be upon us soon for I heard that Eldfjall has erupted, and that is an evil omen," Oskar stated firmly with a solemn face.

"So what exactly is Mortikon? Is he a god?" asked Amber.

"Nay, my child. He was a demigod born of, from the realm of, or sent by Óðin until Agnar slew him in combat. Using the Great Sword of Mjolnir, he was transformed into a leiche, one of the undead. Óðin banished Mortikon from the world, but he is very, very real," said Oskar.

"And who is Agnar? Was he a god too?" asked Anthony.

Oskar chuckled and smiled and said, "Your ancestor. And you are the last living descendant of Agnar! There are consequences, no free rides in life. You, Anthony, were destined to fulfill the prophecies. You can pick whether it is a curse or a blessing."

"Then I choose blessing. I was blessed with Amber! She was part of the destiny, and I don't regard it as a curse," Anthony said, beaming at Amber.

Prior to departing, Oskar had Skuli, Thor, and Hafsteinn swear an oath to never mention the book or Amber and Anthony again. Amber and Anthony bade them good-bye as Oskar led them out of the wizards' tower. "Now I want to see the *real* HearthGlen in person," laughed Amber.

"I need to warn you: don't speak very much as you are outlanders, and spies are everywhere," warned Oskar.

"Yes, we don't want Mortikon after us," stated Anthony solemnly.

Outside the wizards' tower, both Amber and Anthony were like children staring at the proverbial candy jar. Every place had children—playing, laughing children with no care in the world. None of the children were being supervised by parents—there were no pedophiles; no murdering, wandering bums; and no dope-selling junkies. "What has happened to our world?" cried out Amber to Anthony. And to make it better, everyone was smiling. Everyone seemed to live a simple, much better life, greeting folk on the streets and wandering about with contentment.

"Where I came from, *nobody* dared to go outside for fear of being robbed or murdered—not even to mingle with friends, or laugh and make new friends. This is so foreign to me," stated Anthony.

"Ah, but my friends, there is a dark side. We have robberies and murders here too," replied Oskar.

Oskar led them into the shop of a weapons dealer where they obtained a bow, daggers, and a sword for Anthony. They also purchased leather armor for Amber and Anthony. Amber laughed, saying, "I feel silly. Look at me. Why, I can pass for a normal citizen here!" As they exited the shop, they came face to face with a *real* knight clad head to toe in shiny plate armor. *WOW!* thought Anthony, *I never thought in a million years . . .* They eventually came to the Sekhmet area where giant eagles were lined up ready to board passengers.[5] "How the blazes do I ride one of them?" cried Amber. "Where are you taking us now?"

"Why, Agnarborg, of course," said Oskar. "Let me help you up." After Oskar paid the fares, both Amber and Anthony, with the help of Oskar, were straddling one of the eagles. With that, the passenger eagle took to the air. Anthony, with his passenger Amber clinging behind him, was enthralled and also fear-stricken. They had never flown before, not even in their time—let alone riding an eagle. Oskar advised them to not look down to the ground until they get used to it. Anthony was woozy at first because

---

5   Sekhmet: Animals trained as helpers. Birds, lions, cats, etc., were trained to assist people.

it was not only something new, but as the eagle soared up, the ground was falling below. "Whee!" This was fun. The landscape was exquisite. He was really enjoying the excitement of flying. Ahead, there were farms and peasants manning the fields. He had never seen a real farm in his time. "And LOOK! No perimeter fence. HearthGlen has no fence," shouted Anthony. For the first time in his life, he felt a strange contentment in his soul. He had no fear of a government. He was totally free.

"Off to Blesugrof and Fort Hermana," shouted Oskar.

Blesugrof and Hermana

Four hours they flew in the wind, passing farms and grazing livestock. It was now almost October, and the biting, chilly winds were almost icy. It was snowing, so Oskar led the birds over the cloud cover and the snowcapped peaks of Blafjall Mountains. As they neared Blesugrof, Oskar shouted, "Beneath us is the farm, Blesugrof. It is one hundred hectares in size.[6] One of your grandfathers, Agnar, received it from a gnomish king for his service in slaying Mortikon. Do you want to see it?"

"You bet I do! Wow, Agnar got it from a king. I never knew my grandparents," replied Anthony.

They went below the clouds and saw an old woman rounding up sheep. "Here is your great-grandmother now," called out Oskar, pointing toward Anthony's grandmother. She looked up and saw the three riders in the sky and waved at them. With a longing wish, Anthony so badly wanted to land and talk with her; all he could do was to wave back. Oskar waved back and shouted, "You still own Blesugrof, you know. Fort Hermana is just ahead. We will land there and take some rooms in the inn, Boar's Head."

---

[6]   Hectares: About 280 acres.

The three of them landed, retrieved their belongings from the saddlebags from the bird, and headed out toward Boar's Head. Fort Hermana was still a small village now, but not in the time of Amber and Anthony. Like HearthGlen in the future, it was a bustling city, not like this one in the past. The fortress was a nondescript garrison with wooden walls lined with ballistae and armored soldiers. They found the inn, which was a well-kept building with a sign over the door depicting a boar's head. Inside were mounted animal heads, most notably some boars and antlered deer. There were few customers milling around, just enjoying their meals and engaged in conversations. The owner, called Svanhildur, knew Oskar, and they talked while Amber and Anthony looked around.

"Nice place. Let's grab a table in the corner of the room, get some chow and a room for the night," Anthony instructed Oskar.

Oskar replied with a hushed tone, "Remember what I told you: don't speak very much."

Oskar raised his voice and ordered some ale, meat, and bread. "Oh, lest I forget, we need two rooms for the night. We're heading out to Agnarborg tomorrow."

The meal was soon before them, and they were astounded at how the meat tasted so good. Amber took a swig of her ale, crunched her face up, and spewed some onto the table, screeching, "Whoa! That is some strong stuff." She blew a breath from her lips and said, "Tony, take it easy on the ale. It's terribly strong."

Oskar laughed at his friends and said, "If you think this is strong, wait until you try the *landa*."[7]

Anthony laughed in response and added, "What kind of meat is this? I've never had such great meat."

Oskar waved off the remark on the meat and said, "How odd. It is lamb. What kind of meat do you eat in your time? Here, lamb meat is eaten every day. You are strange to me, so alike and yet so different."

"You need to forgive us. We live in a cold, sterile, and uncaring society. I rather enjoy the excitement and newness. Where we come from, the government controls everything in our lives, from our work, transportation, and entertainment to our food," explained Amber.

With that, the meal was consumed, and the trio retired for the night. Anthony and Amber lay in bed and talked about the fresh, clean, and proper society they found themselves in. It still amazed them to think of the new, exciting discoveries they would make every day. "I wonder how this would end. I mean, will we go back to our time, or would we just be sitting in limbo? I, for one, do not look forward to going back to HearthGlen in our time," said Anthony.

---

[7] Landa: A home brew of alcohol, extremely potent. Also known as Black Death, it is made from cheap ingredients.

It was six o'clock in the morning, and the sunrise was not until eight. They left the inn and headed to the boarding area for the birds. Soon they were back in the air, heading for Helgilands. They were heading east, across the seas, and on the shoreline were thousands of seals on the rocks. In the distance, as the sun was breaking the horizon, they could see whales frolicking in the waves. By nine o'clock, they were nearing the shores of Helgilands.

The flight to Agnarborg City took about an hour. They soared over lush green forests, finally landing—but where? There wasn't any city there, and Amber and Anthony were stymied. It wasn't a city—not a city as they knew, but rather, it was built of tree houses! Oskar greeted the small group of elves that had showed up, waving happily.

Anthony shook his head, bewildered as he was. He could only utter, "Why, they look like ME!" He was expecting a typical elf, a Santa Clause elf, the ones who makes presents and cookies. Other than the elongated ears, he looked same as the elves before him.

"You need not worry about spies here. Come and greet your kinfolk, Anthony. I'll find King Rober and introduce you. Oh, and he is a king, so kindly stick to protocol for royalty. He is also one of your grandfathers. His mother is the one we waved at in Blesugrof," said Oskar.

All Anthony could do was to scratch his head and say, "My entire life, my belief systems—my whole world has crashed before me."

Amber laughed and said, "Yours? Safe to say that mine too."

Anthony felt at home. For the first time in his life, he felt a sense of belonging, a purpose in the world. The elves were bombarding both of him and Amber with questions, eager to hear of their escapades. It wasn't long before the small group of elves became a crowd of laughing, smiling elves. The glowing, exuberant enthusiasm of the elves had a choking effect upon him; he was at a loss for words. Oskar and Anthony waded through the crowd and stood before King Rober. Anthony dropped to a knee, Amber as well, and said, "Sire."

King Rober was a dignified, middle-aged, and highly intelligent man with long blond hair. He didn't exude a boorish attitude like other royalties sometimes did but was a down-to-earth person.

"Come, we have much to talk about. Tonight we shall hold a festival in your honor," said the king. The king addressed his subjects. "Please, disperse. Make our guests comfortable. You all will meet them in due course. Everyone will meet at the festival."

The four of them walked to the Tree of Life, which was Rober's castle, and entered it.

Friða, the kings' wife, and his children welcomed their guests with open arms. "I see you are a human. The king's mother is also of the human race. I notice that you too of mixed blood, Anthony!. I humbly bid you welcome within our coven."

Amber blushed toward Friða and replied warmly, "Thank you. You're too kind."

"I-I never knew that I was an elf until Oskar told me. You need to forgive me, as I am at a loss for words," said Anthony.

"How strange, not knowing you are an elf. A good thing you aren't an orc," added Friða laughingly.

The king led the group into the meeting chamber, where Oskar retold the couple's harrowing escape from the future. Anthony carried the book in a knapsack, and he needed a way to destroy it. The king was astonished to hear that Mortikon was still wielding power amidst the humans, but he wasn't surprised. "The world is evil, and Mortikon will not be easily defeated," interjected the king. "As for your boon, we can offer you some assistance, but not much. For you see, Traikon is not here, but I know where to find him. I'm afraid that you are diving into perilous waters because your task takes you into the Northern Realm, the lair of Mortikon and his minions."

Anthony thought for a few seconds and said, "Northern Realm, where is that? This all new to us. Perhaps someone can show us where to go."

Oskar added, "I am forbidden to enter the Northern Realm. As a guardian, Óðin has instructed us not to interfere, not even to touch the grounds of the Northern Realm."

"What or who is a guardian?" asked Anthony with a quizzed face.

The king squinted and replied, "Guardians are sent by the gods to assist us in perilous times. They used to be called Referees."

Anthony dropped a shoulder and, in amazement asked, "A-are you a god? L-like immortal and stuff?" and turned to Amber as if to help him to comprehend.

"Nay, my friend, they are as mortal as you are. Helgi the Great helped us escape from the humans, but he was assassinated for his trouble," retorted King Rober.

Anthony was scratching his head in bewilderment. "Now I *really* am confused. I never believed in gods or religion and such, and now you are saying that Oskar is from the gods, but he isn't a god?"

Oskar answered Anthony. "Everyone has a purpose in this world. Let me just say that everyone has a station in this life. There are greater powers in this cosmos that you will never fathom. The book is one of them. Yes, I am from the gods, and I am as mortal as you."

Anthony asked if they could sit down as he could see that his whole world was dissolving before his own eyes. *Gnomes, elves, giant birds, magic, Mortikon, Traikon, and guardians. What kind of madness is this?* thought Anthony. He cupped his hands over his face and shut his eyes as to make everything go back to normal. "Then Jesus was a guardian. He was from the gods. He was killed for it. Is that what you are saying?"

"Aye, as was Hitler in your times and Stalin and Gandhi. They were all guardians," replied Oskar.

Anthony threw his hands in the air and said, "I need to think."

"Aye. Perhaps we all need some time to think. I will fulfill your boon as much as I can," said the king. "We shall speak more about this when you arrive for the festival."

Amber and Anthony were outside of the Tree of Life and sitting around the campfire. It was seven o'clock when the festivities started, and already, the cool October night had a slight chill in the air. The entire coven turned out for the gala, and of course, the king, queen, and their children were there as well. There were elves everyplace, in the trees, on the ground, and wandering around the bushes. They were dressed regally, with flowers in their hair, dancing around the campfire. Everyone was laughing and singing along with the orchestra. The band was consisted of lute players, pipers, drummers, and oboe players. "So, Friða, tell me more about this coven. I'm fascinated by them," requested Amber.

Friða acquiesced and said, "Well, we are of the Wood Elves clan, and the other clan is of the Dark Elves. There are a few of the Dark Elves here tonight. We elves do not intermingle with the humans, of course. Over there," she said, pointing to the left, "is

Laugalfur, a warrior from the coven. He was tortured in a dungeon by the humans." She was thinking of the time when humans ruled.

"Oh my. We too have similar tales of mistreating others in my time," Amber responded.

Anthony turned to King Rober and asked, "Shall we discuss our quest, Your Highness?"

"But of course. I was thinking of asking the dwarfs to send a warrior. And the gnomes too. You will need all the help you can get. In my younger years, I too was tasked with helping Traikon on a different quest. Traikon is my father-in-law, by the way," responded the king.

With a strange look on his face, Anthony said, "Oh, Traikon. Is he an elf?"

Chuckling, the king laughed and said, "Well, difficult to say. He is a demon wizard, but a wonderful demon. When he is in his human form, he is a marvelous being. In his dragon form, he helped us little people in the revolt against the humans."

Anthony no longer marveled at the magical events around him; he now took things at face value. "And where is Traikon now, may I ask?"

"In the volcano called Eldfjall," stated the king.

Anthony thought a second and said, "So that's where the nightmares were coming from. I kept dreaming of Traikon and Mortikon. So that is the connection between Eldfjall, Traikon, and Mortikon."

"Yes," interjected Oskar. "Your task is to return to Eldfjall and heave the book into the lava below."

Training

Both Amber and Anthony were quartered in the Tree of Life, in a section off the main branch where they could had a view from above of the stupendous balcony. Oskar had departed to StrompurForge City to assist them in their quest, and they spent the time chatting with the other members of the coven. In the meantime, Friða's mother, Gjaldakona, called on the two, wanting to meet the two outlanders. She was a real hag—a honest witch—with stooped shoulders, straggly hair, and disgusting wart on her nose with a single black hair protruding from it. She was dressed in typical all-black witches' attire, and she had a horrible cackle when she spoke, which brought about the kind of feeling people get when they run their fingernails over a chalkboard. But she was the most gentle, lively, and lovely person you could ever meet. She was sitting next to the kitchen table and she advised, "Ye needs some training. I knows from me experiences. Dost thou have four, maybe five months afore winter ends? When Mortikon strikes there will be no sparing of lives. Ye needs to be inside the Northern Realms afore that."

She sent shivers down the backs of Amber and Anthony, mostly for focusing on her nose! Amber thought to herself, *She is one ugly woman. How did such a lovely girl as Friða have had such a hideous mother?*

Four days had elapsed, and suddenly, there came a knock on the door. Outside stood Oskar and a small dwarf who was dressed in full plate armor. The dwarf had long red hair and a beard, and he had a bulbous nose. His eyes were like small sunken black orbs topped by thick red eyebrows.

"Come in. Please, do come in." Anthony greeted his guests. "We talked with Gjaldakona the other day, and she said that we have little time until Mortikon strikes. Four, maybe five months."

Oskar nodded and said, "This is Kæsar from StrompurForge. He will be training you in weapon skills. In a day or so, we will have a gnome here to train you as a rogue. He will be deceptive. Don't let his size fool you. These skills you will need if you plan to return from the evil lands."

"Aye, we dunna 'ave no much time. I be a paladin by trade and will teach ye healing and swordsmanship," said Kæsar. "King Rober 'twas a fine rogue in his time. His brother, Prince Stefan, will be here a' morrow ta greets ye, though he never 'came no warrior."

They spent the time getting to know Kæsar and what would be expected of them during the training. Of course, Gjaldakona dropped by, as well as King Rober and Queen Friða, and spent several hours talking about the time of Anthony and Amber, who recollected how sterile society had become in the future and talked about the rebels.

"King Rober and I were rebels before we came to these lands," said Friða. "Those were perilous times."

Anthony and Amber were ready for their training, and they were waiting for the gnome trainer and Stefan to show up. Over longleaf tea with Kæsar, they were deciding who would receive which training from whom. Amber was excited about being a rogue, and Anthony would receive paladin training, so it became a dead issue. The tea was excellent, and the trio spent the rest of the time talking about what it was to be from the future. Soon afterward, both and the gnome and Stefan arrived, and after exchanging greetings, they got down to business concerning the quest. The gnome, named Gagns, said that it was good to be training Amber because she was such a lovely woman. Gagns, almost four feet tall, was a funny character with thick, bushy bluish eyebrows, a short haircut, and a smile that drove gnomish women wild. Sporting leather for armor, he was a fine specimen for a gnome. Prince Stefan was a spitting image of the king. He was a year younger than the king, physically fit and smart as a whip.

"I once did a similar quest with my brother, the king, and I too had to endure training like yours. But I only received training in swordsmanship. I don't envy you. Lots of training and I still have the aches and pains from it," stated Stefan. "I shall convey my magical sword upon you. You will need it." Turning toward Amber, he said, "You know, Amber, my mother is a human like you."

"I won't go easy on ye," said Gagns. "Yer a fine lady, but it dunna gets ya a break fer it. Ye will do just fine though."

With that, the training commenced, and it was hard on both Amber and Anthony. They received plenty of bruises, aches, and pains for their reward. Day after day, they were up at five o'clock and trained until nine o'clock in the evening. Anthony received swordsmanship training plus healing powers. Amber learned how to steal, got stealth powers, and was trained to use daggers. They had one day a week to recuperate and, and rest they did! October waned, and November, with its cold, wintery, blustery season made them miserable. December fell upon them, where it was total darkness twenty-four hours a day. Amber enjoyed that time of the year as the northern lights were fantastic to watch. The night skies were aflame with colors of orange, blue, purple, and green. Watching the bursts of the Northern Lights dancing in the sky was awe-inspiring. It was like they could reach up and pull them out of the heavens; they seemed so real. But there was snow—a lot of snow. And with the snow came its kith and kin, the cold. January came in like a lion, with constant winds howling, never ceasing. February followed January, mostly same as the previous month. The training was constant and grueling, but it kept on, with secretive reports of the spies from the north further their desires for the training.

Finally, the training concluded. Now began the planning for the quest's route. Stefan had used the same route on his quest many years ago, and he suggested the same course be used. Everyone involved offered their own opinion: Oskar, the king, Stefan, and Gjaldakona.

"'Tis soon be March. The snows be gone soon, and ye be easy to get to Eldfjall," said Gjaldakona. "Gotta keep an eye in the sky. Scryers be thick and wraith riders too."

"Aye, right you are, Gjaldakona. My father, Ambassador Runar, tells me that Mortikon thinks you will be passing the Lava Gates on your journey. The wraith riders are even now scouring the Blafjall Mountains to the east. I suggest that you use the same path, up toward Outpost Bleakness, then turn to your east," advised King Rober.

"Aye," added Kæsar. "Get over the Mountains. 'N keep a eye fer Konglos, 'n orcs 'n yeti."

"My father will try to keep Mortikon and Prince Maura busy. Sanctuary City can try to put sanctions in place. He is the ambassador to Sanctuary City watching over the elves. But I warn you, if Mortikon catches a trace of the book, then open war will be upon us," said Stefan. "Here, you take this, my looking glass. It was valuable when I went questing."

"T-thank you. I don't know if we are up to this task, but I will try not to fail you," said Anthony. "But if we succeed, how do we come back here?"

"Traikon will see to it," stated Gjaldakona with a cackle.

"Ye needs some supplies, but go easy on 'em. You canna carry much 'n I'm 'fraid it won't be 'nuff," said Gagns.

"Is anyone else coming? What happens if we run into trouble?" queried Amber.

"Nay, ye be alone. There be no help either," declared Gjaldakona. "Succeed 'n all be well. Fail 'n the world be in chaos."

Anthony turned to Amber with a look of pain that seemed to come from the pit of his stomach—the whole world now rested on their shoulders.

The Quest

The day had come. There would be no turning around now for the world was on the brink of disaster. The enemy's spies had been working overtime, gathering information about the whereabouts of the book. Once the enemy's forces or Anthony and Amber reach the mainland, it will be a do-or-die situation. Boar's Head Inn reported that an unusual number of men had been questioned about anyone named Anthony. Rumor was that anyone with information about Anthony would be rewarded. The sentries stationed at Fort Hermana had informed the elven spies that flying wraith riders were spotted over the mountains to the north. Occasionally, the scryers were observed off to the east. Mortikon was desperately seeking Anthony. They were certain that orc patrols were increased on the Northern Realm's side of the border.

Gagns was saying good-bye to Amber. He gave her a magic dagger, a rather rare weapon that he had used to dispatch many foes in the past. "I wanna give it to ye. Ye be a fine student o' mine 'n a mighty pretty lass too. It be magic. Use it 'n your foes canna stop bleeding."

"Well, thank you for teaching me. I'll not forget you as long as I live," replied Amber. And she meant it too. She would never forget the excitement of knowing gnomes and learning first hand that they really existed in the world.

Gagns motioned her down toward him, and when she did bow down, he kissed her on the cheek. She blushed and said, "With all my heart, I will cherish the dagger to the end of my days." Her eyes bore into him with sadness, which caused his to eyes water. He knew that they would never meet again.

Kæsar extended a hand toward Anthony and said, "May the gods be with you. Perhaps we be meetin' in Valhalla. I hope so."[8]

"I hope so too. You have been a terrific teacher. I-if only we had more time to be true friends," choked Anthony. "I hate good-byes. Let's just say till next time."

Both Amber and Anthony had tears welling up in their eyes as they waved good-bye. They knew that they would never encounter their friends again. Amber turned with a sad look on her face, cleared her throat, and said, "Let's go to the final briefing," and let it stand at that.

King Rober, Oskar, and Prince Stefan were making preparations for Anthony and Amber to leave. It was decided that they should board a schooner that

---

[8] Valhalla: The Viking heaven.

would land the party just east of Sko Forest at a fishing village called Fiskurmin. That way, they could skirt Fort Hermana and avoid the spies in the area.

"Do you have enough health potions, mage bandages, flaxen bread, and water?" asked the king.

"Yes, sire, we have enough for three weeks if we ration them. And I have the weapons and telescope as well," replied Anthony.

"And you have the maps?" added Stefan.

"That and the book, Your Highness," declared Amber.

"Very well, I wish you success with the task lying ahead. May the gods be with you," stated the king.

Both Amber and Anthony somberly bid everyone good-bye, and they jumped into the cart that would carry them to the port.

It was about a two-hour trip over bumpy roads on the horse-driven cart, with the two of them riding mostly in silence. They knew that the world would change regardless of the outcome of their adventure. Somehow, they both knew that Mortikon would press on with his desire to own the book. Perhaps not in this time, but surely in the future. "I wonder often about destiny. I was a loser back in our time, but now that the fate of the world is in our hands . . ." uttered Anthony.

"Tony, what in the world makes you say that? You aren't a loser. Not in my eyes. And we *will* succeed. I just know it," retorted Amber.

Soon the cart discharged the passengers and left them standing before the schooner. *Lady Heppin* was the name of the schooner, and it was a magnificent ship. The dwarven captain greeted Anthony and Amber as the two of them were led to their cabins. The crew, which was comprised of gnomes and elves, were a hardy lot. It was obvious that sea life had weathered them as they were tanned and muscular. Overhead, Anthony and Amber could see hundreds of seagulls diving into the water in search of a meal and crying songs in the air.

"Ye be matter o' two days till we reach Fiskurmin," advised the captain of the *Lady Heppin*. "We be a-castin' off here in a hour."

"Thank you, Captain. Are you sure that you can trust the crew? A bit of grog makes folk talk," asked Anthony.

"Aye. We be dwarfs, elves, and gnomes. We dunna talk to humans," responded the captain. "When you land, get outta the village, and then, ye be on yer own."

It wasn't long before they hoisted the anchors and cast off. It was horrible because as soon as they hit the breakwaters of the port, Anthony and Amber both became ill to the gills. The ship was lurching to and fro. Each wave caused their stomachs to churn. The gale-force winds didn't help much either, and they both hung their heads over the bow, throwing up constantly. The crew laughed and said "landlubbers," which made Anthony and Amber feel queasy, and they ran back to the bow and threw up again. They both refused to go to their cabin. They wanted to breathe the icy, air, which made them feel better. They couldn't eat anything because they couldn't hold it down. Whining and feeling sorry for themselves only made matters worse. After eight hours of misery, they stumbled to their cabin and fell asleep.

The next day was better. The winds had died down a bit. "I'll never take a boat trip again as long as I live," declared Anthony.

"And I'll never be a seaman for all the money in the world," laughed Amber.

The creaking of the ship's timbers became natural to them; it was a part of seafaring. Every time a wave would hit the ship, it would lurch and sing its creaking song. The seagulls never abandoned the ship; they were a constant between Helgilands and the mainland. It wasn't long before the man in the crow's nest yelled down, "Land ho!"

The captain sought out the two and said, "We be soon a-landin'. Mind what I said afore. Get outta the village as soon as ya can."

"Aye-aye, Captain," responded Anthony.

It was long before the ship had entered the breakwaters of the port. Anthony and Amber were busy retrieving their possessions and gearing up for the landing. After disembarking, Anthony turned and looked at the ship swarming with longshoremen. He saluted to the captain, turned to Amber, and said, "We're on our own now."

It was dark now, and it started to snow. Under the cover of snowflakes, they made their way into Sko Forest. As they pushed farther into the woods, the lights from the village dimmed until they ceased to shine. There were strange sounds from the forest: the hooting of owls, the howling from a distant wolf, and the rustling of deer that were out foraging. The night afforded no assistance from its moonless sky in trying to determine where they were. They had decided to camp for the night but without a campfire lest they were detected. "I'll take the first watch," said Anthony. "Four-hour watches. We don't want any surprises."

Sunrise was almost ten o'clock at this time of the year, and sunset was about one o'clock in the afternoon. "When we can find out where we are, then we can set our next leg of the journey," replied Amber.

The next day, Anthony climbed a huge tree to orient them before pushing ahead. Using his folding telescope, he located the Blafjall Mountains. After judging that the two of them were heading north, he adjusted their journey to the east. It appeared to be about twenty miles distant from them, using the rising sun as a direction finder. He scampered down and said, "Looks like a storm's blowing toward us. Let's grab some chow and get some distance from here. Hopefully, we can make lean-to for protection. Maybe twenty miles to the mountain."

"OK, I hope we can find a cave or something, make a fire. During daylight it won't be a big problem, but at night, it will be a dead giveaway," advised Amber. "How long do you think it would take to cover the twenty miles?"

"Oh, I suppose a day or two. Pretty rough in this wilderness, what with climbing fallen logs and crossing the streams we encounter on the way," responded Anthony.

They sat down and shared a bit of flaxen bread with a cup of water. Every once in a while, they could hear ravens in the treetops. "If you can't hear the birds, it's a sign that something is afoot," said Amber. "I learned it in training: concentrate on the little details of your environment."

They adjusted their direction to the east and commenced their hike. Up, around, and down as they trudged through the forests. The progress they made was little compared to what they needed.

"I hope there are not any wolves or yeti. I heard from Gagns that yetis like to congregate in the tree lines of mountains. And at this time of the year, we've got to be careful of avalanches," said Amber.

"Yeah, I heard of 'em. Wolves, I mean. Last night but off in the distance," professed Anthony. "As for the yeti, aren't they the abominable?"

"Right you are, Tony. I don't want to meet up with one either," stated Amber.

For hours, they stayed the course until Anthony said he wanted to check on their bearings. He scaled a tree and said they needed to go to the left. After descending the tree, he advised that they should press on for about two more hours and then pitch camp. "We're about three-eights of the way there. I'll take first watch when we get there."

The two them picked a spot that afforded the best defensive position within the forest. Since it was dark, a campfire was not available. Nevertheless, they ate some flaxen bread and washed the meal down with water from a nearby stream. "You know, Kæsar said that when we run out of food, we should forage for pine cones. They are great if you want to take the nuts from them. The taste is OK if you can get over the sap from the cones," said Anthony. "That and the wild mushrooms, but you gotta be careful to pick the nonpoisonous ones."

"I didn't know that," replied Amber. "I guess survival skills will come in handy."

They retired for the night, with Anthony taking the lead watch.

First Encounters

Amber woke Anthony up and said, "We gotta get going." The storm yesterday passed them by, probably because of the high peaks of the mountain. "We won't be lucky again. The clouds sure do look black and gloomy."

"Yep. Let's grab a bite to eat and head out," responded Anthony.

It was the same old story. The going was slow and monotonous, having to skirt fallen trees and cross streams. Eventually, they reached the tree line of the mountains, and Anthony perused the map, trying to figure out the best way to the mountain pass. The sun was setting, and they wanted to put the trek in the history books. Ahead of them was a stream, teeming with jumping salmon fishes. "Let me see now. Seems like there will be a waterfall up ahead. Must be about seven miles away. But beyond that is the old road to Bleakness," said Anthony. The sunset was spectacular with the background of the mountain. They could see where the frost line was receding; the melting snows were swelling the streams. They pushed ahead, making about two miles, when all of a sudden Anthony's magic sword began to hum and give off a blue hue. Trouble ahead!

His sword gave off a warning whenever foes were in the vicinity. Amber switched to her stealth mode; she became invisible. Whispering, he instructed her to scout the area while he maintained cover. Anthony was on edge, his heartbeat raced, and he waited for anything to appear from nothingness.

Ahead of Amber was an orc, brown skinned and with two huge fangs protruding from his lower jaw. He was struggling with a goblin that was chained by the neck. "You little runt, I said to keep up the pace!" screamed the orc. With that, the orc pulled hard on the chain, and the goblin was pulled from his feet.

"M-master, no hurt me," cried the goblin as the orc began to pummel him. The goblin was dressed in a loincloth, and his skinny, elongated arms were funny to see. Looking for any more orcs in case there were others, Amber maintained her stealth mode but found no other orcs. As she turned to return to Anthony, she stepped on a twig. The cracking wood alerted the orc. Amber lost her concentration, which was needed for using the stealth mode, and immediately, the surprised orc drew his weapon and charged Amber. Anthony immediately broke his cover and, with sword in hand, charged. The orc took a swipe at Amber with his sword, but it found nothing but empty air. Her training had increased her agility, and she easily sidestepped the attack. The orc parried her daggers and struck Amber with his shield. She staggered, and the screaming orc went in for the kill! Anthony leapt into the battle, catching the orc off guard. The orc was wounded by Anthony's sword. Amber regained her footing and drove her daggers deep into the back of the orc! Hollering in pain, the orc was no match for the heroes and slumped to the ground.

Anthony ran toward Amber and shrieked, "You all right?" He could see that she was bleeding from the shield smash to her head.

"I'll be OK once my head clears. I'll have to be careful next time. I lost my concentration and *boom*, no stealth," she said.

Anthony laid his hands on Amber in order to heal her, which didn't take much time.

The goblin, cowering out of fear, cried, "No hurt, master, no hurt." He was trying to fend off any other attacks from the strange beings before him. The goblin, who had a greenish hue to his skin and huge round eyes, had been crying from the beating. He was a strange creature, with two thin hairs on his head. It was skinny as a rail and had bulbous knees and overgrown feet. It began to grovel at Anthony's feet.

Anthony picked up the chain from the ground and immediately got a response from the goblin: "It burns! Master, it burns!"

Amber asked, "What next? We don't want to make him our prisoner, and the orcs will be told of us if we let him go."

"Wow, I never thought about that," said Anthony. "Just what do with him now?" He turned to the goblin and asked his name.

"M-my name?" the goblin stared back toward Anthony. "Me be called Stemni," the goblin answered.

"All right, Stemni. What do you propose we do with you? The orcs will be upon us if we cut you free," demanded Anthony.

"Oh no, I not tell orcs. I hate orcs. Orcs make slave of me," responded Stemni. With his huge blinking eyes, he cracked a smile that revealed razor-sharp teeth and pleaded for his freedom.

"Amber, search the dead orc. See if he has a key to the neck brace," instructed Anthony. "Now, promise me that you will not tell the orcs. Promise or I won't turn you free," Anthony demanded Stemni.

"I promise," replied Stemni, pleading away, "I promise."

Amber returned with the key and commenced to remove the shackles on his neck. "Hold still! I can't cut you free with you fidgeting around."

With the chain gone, Stemni did somersaults and laughed, saying in a child's voice, "I be free! Thank, master."

"Off with you, Stemni. You're free, go back where you came from," said Anthony.

To that, Stemni said, "Back? To where? I live here."

"Well, stay away from the orcs then," retorted Anthony.

Stemni just blinked his eyes and didn't move. With a questioning face, Anthony said, "Well? Go! Scram! You're free to leave."

Stemni thought for a second and said, "What mean *scram*?"

Anthony chuckled and replied, "Get outta here," and waved his hand to say good-bye.

Anthony fished out his map to see how much longer it would take to get to the pass. Stemni stared at Anthony and asked, "What's that?"

"A map," replied Anthony.

"Map? What's a map?" asked Stemni.

"You mean you don't know what a map is?" asked Anthony incredulously. "It shows where things are. Look over here," he said, pointing his finger to Eldfjall. "Here is where we are going, to the volcano."

"I can help. I know where orcs are. And Queen Konglos too. I show the way," proudly stated Stemni. Then he added, "You need my help? Orcs close by. I show you the way."

Amber laughed and said, "Well, they said we wouldn't get any help. A busybody of a goblin is better than no help. What do you think? And I don't relish the idea of getting orcs on us."

Anthony pursed his lips and thought for a few seconds and said, "OK. Show me on the map where the orcs and Konglos are at. But once we get past the mountains, you can scram, got it?"

Stemni led the two of them to the waterfall. It was just in time for it started sleeting and hailing. Stemni had gotten some distance between him and the two, and he turned, waving, and said, "Come!

You come. Quickly, master, come." He directed them to a path behind the cascading wall of water, where they couldn't talk because of the deafening roar of the falls. *At least we're out of the storm. But are we out of the fire or not?* thought Anthony. The cavern was much bigger than they had expected, and as the deafening sound diminished, they pushed deeper into the cave. The cavern was slick from the waters, as well as dank and clammy. There were plenty of wild mushrooms growing here and there. The mildew and moisture only added to the atmosphere of gloom. When they finally came to a reasonably quiet area in the cave, Anthony instructed them to make camp for the night. He wanted to wait out the storm, get his bearings, and rest. At least here, they didn't have to post a guard. The three of them fell asleep as soon their heads hit their knapsacks. *That was really quite a day,* thought Anthony as he crept into a slumber.

Anthony woke up with a yawn, stretching his arms to wake up his body. Suddenly, he was jolted to his senses. *Where are the books?* In a panic, he scanned the cavern, and then he realized they were underneath him. *Whew,* thought Anthony, *Without these books . . .* He saw Amber sitting by the campfire, and he greeted her warmly. She was eating fish, and he suddenly realized he was famished. "Where did you get the fish?" he asked.

Amber smiled and said, "Stemni, of course! This is the best fish I've had in my whole life. Have some, my darling Tony."

He dug in like there was no tomorrow, and between bites, he remarked that it was good. "Where is the pesky Stemni anyway?" he inquired.

"Oh, he went to catch more fish. He won't be long," responded Amber. "Why did you call him pesky? He really makes my day with his innocence and his childlikeness. He is so adorable."

Anthony paused for a second and said, "Oh, just a figure of speech, I guess." Then he let out a chuckle. "I kind of enjoy having him around, but you know that when we get over the mountains, he's history. Sad to say it too, so don't get attached to him."

Amber had a forlorn look on her face, and she said, "Yes. I wish we could teach him things. I laughed when he didn't know what a map was and *scram*. He is so innocent and sweet."

Anthony, changing the subject, asked her how long she had been awake and if she had explored the cave.

"I suppose that I was up about two hours ago, and to answer to your question, yes," answered Amber. "The way out over the mountains will be about a two-hour trek, but the climb down will be hazardous. Going on with our original plan, would have run into orc patrols, not to mention the queen, Konglos. Stemni's way will overpass the orcs and spiders."

Stemni returned to the camp with a flopping fish in his mouth. Amber and Anthony greeted him warmly with smiles on their faces. "Are enjoying the fish?" inquired Anthony.

Stemni took a bite of the fish, swallowed it, and replied, "Fishes is fish." The two of them watched as Stemni finished his fish and said, "We go now? My home up," as he pointed toward the roof of the cave.

"What do you mean your home is up. Do you mean on top of the mountain?" asked Anthony.

"Nay, here up. I'll show you," replied the goblin.

Stemni's loping stride was strange. Using his feet and hands to move along, led the group farther into the darkness of the cavern, stopped, and pointing to a hoist said, "Here. Come, master."

In front of them was a hoist of wooden planks big enough to fit five people. They hopped on, and hoisted themselves up, pulling hand over hand on the rope. After they had winched upward for three hundred feet, they left the elevator when Stemni startled the group, saying, "This way! Come, master." He led them into a dark corridor with musty, stale air. It must have been thirty feet wide. The walls were decked out with ancient torches every twenty yards. Whoever carved out passage must have had help from dwarfs. Eventually they found the exit, and before them was an abandoned village within the cavern. "Here, master. My home," said Stemni with obvious pride.

Anthony and Amber were scanning the buildings, and they found remnants of Norse writings, adding to the suspicions that the creators were dwarfs. Anthony turned to Stemni and asked, "Do you live here alone? Where did everyone go?"

Stemni blinked his huge eyes and said, "They left me."

Amber felt perturbed at that, being abandoned here alone, left to fend for his own survival.

"Oh, I am so sorry. No wonder you wouldn't run off when we released you. But why did they abandon you?"

Stemni paused for a moment and replied, "I was stealing. I took taters and food from the orcs. When I came back, they were gone." The feeling of sadness quickly faded, and he beamed at Amber, saying, "Come. This way. Mountaintop this way," as he pointed to the right.

"Perhaps," added Anthony, "we should make camp here. It will be dark soon, and we don't need to stumble around in the gloom of night. Besides, I want to see your home."

That night, Amber and Anthony discussed about having to leave Stemni behind. "Poor fella, being abandoned once again. Tony, I can't do that to him again. He is so childlike it breaks my heart," she said.

"I know, and I feel your anguish. But I don't know what to do with him. You knew that when the time comes, we have to say good-bye," responded Anthony.

"Y-yeah, but he is so alone in the world. Maybe Traikon will take him in. That would make all the difference for him," said Amber despondently.

"Amber," said Anthony starkly.

"Please, Tony? With sugar on top, please," she pleaded.

Feeling remorse, he caved in and said, "OK, I'll ask Traikon when we get to the volcano."

Amber hugged Anthony and showered him with kisses.

In the morning, they talked with Stemni about their decision. "How would you like to go with us to the volcano? I mean we can try to get you back to where your family is."

When Stemni heard that, he yelled "WHOOPEE" and began to flip somersaults in the air!

"Home. My fadur, my modur," he said, obviously delirious in excitement. "Come, quickly, master. Home, WHOOPEE."

Amber was beaming with joy and said happily, "Do you need things to take with you? I mean, we won't be back, you know."

"Nay, I don't be needing nothing. Come. Let us leave," Stemni responded smiling.

The trio picked up their belongings, and Anthony led with an "OK then, let's be off." All of them left the abandoned village walking on air. Perhaps it was the right thing to do—at least, their remorse was gone. They took an uphill path that would take them to the top of the mountain. It was a winding, rising path that took over an hour to reach, but eventually, the trio espied the exit from the cave. As they neared the exit, the winds picked up as the cavern behind them was sucking air from the skies. The top of the mountain was upon them.

On the Top of the World

The view before them was panoramic. They could see for miles in every direction, and the mountains were crowned with snowcapped peaks that gave off colors such as baby-blue hues and white. At this altitude, their breaths came out as frozen air. Below them, they could see the tops of the clouds, and between the clouds they could see the landscape beneath. Their eyes were drawn toward the hulking volcano in the distance. Ominous black swirling clouds danced in a circle around the volcano. Occasionally, there was a flash of lightning emitted from Eldfjall. There was a few seconds of silence, followed by grumbling as the sound of the thunder reached their ears.

"What an awesome sight. See over there, Stemni. That's where we are going," said Amber.

With a disinterested attitude, Stemni shrugged his shoulders and said, "I see before."

But for Anthony and Amber, it was all new. They had never seen the view from a mountain, just skyscrapers and man-made structures. Anthony fished out his telescope and scanned all directions, the skies, and the mountains. He wanted to be sure not to be surprised by winged wraith riders or yetis.

His view of the surrounding peaks was jolted by some wraith riders off in the distance.

"We need to get off of this plateau. Wraiths in the distance," advised Anthony. "From now on, we need to keep a sharp eye out." The trio, led by Stemni, descended a path that had been whittled from the mountain, probably by dwarfs. "Keep your balance. One slip and you will wind up falling to your deaths," advised Anthony. "Lots of snow and ice. I'll feel better once we get to firm ground."

On they descended, toward the frost line of the mountain. It was monotonous going, climbing boulders, leaping cracks, and scampering in and out of the ravines. Occasionally, they could hear the cries of the eagles as they perched in the ledges. Soon they were breaking the cloud barrier. The clouds there were nothing but mist, and soon everyone was drenched. With the misty clouds came wind chills. There was no escaping for the interlopers, and they were soon slapping their arms to try and increase the blood flow. "I-it will be d-dark s-soon. L-let's f-find a c-cave," instructed a freezing Anthony. The frozen trio soon found a cave that afforded safety from the elements. But with no campfire, all they could do was to huddle up and wait for daybreak. It was a miserable night. The sound of their chattering teeth was horrible.

Anthony declined the flaxen bread when they woke up. The only thing on his mind was to get to firm ground. On they descended, half slipping and falling, half on their feet. But they had entered the frost line, and the warmer winds picked up their spirits. When the clouds were over them, they could see the landscape below. It was a barren and bleak picture: mostly cooled lava fields from the volcano and not a tree in sight. There were the usual geysers spouting high toward the heavens and the occasional *rjupan*. "If we can catch a few of the birds, then we'd have meat with the bread," said Anthony. The tundra was teeming with animal life: foxes, birds, fishes in the streams, and of course, yetis. The trio welcomed the sight, as the miserable night in the cave was still fresh in their minds. On they trudged as the ground ahead loomed before them.

"A few more hours, then we can try to settle in a cave, dry ourselves out. Maybe we'll spend the night there," advised Anthony.

The gang finally had reached terra firma, and soon, they found a suitable cave to be used as shelter. Stemni went outside, searching for stuff for a campfire, and returned with damp marsh reeds and yeti scat. Finally, the trio was sitting around the campfire, naked as could be, drying out their clothes. The campfire smoked as it started, but eventually the smoke disappeared as the roaring flames engulfed the kindling. The yeti scat stunk, but since it made excellent fuel, they soon got used to it. The group was soon comfortable enough with their environment and talked about their adventures; the couple invited Stemni to join the conversation. Eventually, Stemni offered to catch some fish from the nearby stream and gather up some *rjupan* eggs. Soon they were eating a hearty meal, and when their clothes were dry, they donned them. With stomachs full, they were overcome with doziness, and soon, they were sound asleep. Of course, Anthony had the knapsack under him, using it as a pillow.

It was daybreak. The glowing orb in the sky was beginning its trek across the heavens. Anthony was using his telescope to see if any villains were nearby, and Stemni was foraging for eggs in the tundra while Amber was stirring with the new dawn.

"Mornin'," said Anthony. "Looks like a wonderful day ahead of us. We should arrive at Eldfjall sometime around Easter. A great of time of the year, what with the renewal of life in nature."

Amber ran her fingers through her hair, cocked her head, and said "Morning" in return. "Where is Stemni?" she asked.

"Out to get some food for us," Anthony replied. "I checked out the skies and the slopes, and it seems to be OK. But things can change in a heartbeat."

After the meal, the three of them began their trek anew. They were constantly scanning the skies overhead for dreadful wraith riders, and they kept to the ravines and gullies to avoid detection as the hours progressed by. Every now and then, the intruders would kick up some nesting *svala* and scurried to avoid the onslaught of the birds' bombardment. The landscape went from passable to almost unacceptable due to the *myri* and its swamplike ground.[9] They had to backtrack to find a detour around it, which meant lost time. Stemni, because of his small stature, went ahead of Amber and Anthony to search for a way through the *myri*. The putrid waters carried the scent of decaying matter, and there was also a sulfurous smell in the air. Their hair and clothes were mired in mud, and because of it, the exhausted trio hoped to find their way quickly through the swamplike environment. Eventually, they found the end of the *myri*, and they stepped onto solid ground again. They rested for about ten minutes before continuing their journey, hoping to make up for lost time. They turned to the east as they need to find some cover and concealment for the night. The group found a cave in the foothills of Blafjall Mountains and camped there after Amber, using her stealth powers, surveyed the cave to be sure there wasn't any yeti.

Cold and exhausted, the trio rested a bit before they started a campfire. They were careful to not make a large fire, as it was dark by then. Anthony said, "I'll be glad to see a real bed again," to which Amber laughed and added, "It would be great to sleep in my own bed. Sure beats sleeping on twigs." Both of them were perplexed about the outcome of their quest. "Will we remain here, in this time? What's to be of us?" mused Amber. "I mean is there

---

9   Myri: Bog or swamplike terrain.

a portal or something to get back home? Not that I relish going back, but what exactly is our destinies?"

"Amber, I just don't know. I mean everything I ever thought, learned, dreamed of is smashed to bits. Maybe Traikon will give us guidance when we get there," conjectured Anthony.

Sunrise was a welcome sight that elevated their spirits. They left the shelter of the cave, and all of a sudden, Anthony's sword sounded the alarm! With a screech from above, a wraith rider assailed them. Razor sharp claws dug into Anthony's shoulder, causing a blinding rush of pain. Stemni leapt onto the dragonlike bird, sinking his teeth into its back, while Amber sank her daggers into its ribs. The wraith rider, dislodged by the attack, strode into battle with swords aflame. The wraith was no match for the three of them as Anthony chopped off the leg of the offending claw using his sword. By then, the rider was involved in hand-to-hand battle with Amber. Stemni jumped from the bird to the humanoid and began gnawing on the riders' leg. Between the screeching and cries of pain from Anthony, it was pandemonium. Amber managed to dodge, with the help from Stemni, the rider's thrust. In turn, she buried her dagger deep into his back. Anthony finished the rider with a blow to the head from his sword.

Lying on the ground, Anthony began to use his healing powers on himself while asking everyone if they were all right. Stemni just stared at Anthony for a moment and said, "Bad rider." Amber was fishing for a mage bandage in her knapsack as she said, "Let's get you fixed up, and then let's get outta here. There might be more of them."

"Agreed," said Anthony.

Ogres, Trolls, Orcs, and Things That Go Bump in the Night

General Snagtann and Prince Maura were summoned by the Sanctuary City Ruling Counsel because of the unrest in the border areas. They were sitting in their chairs, listening to the delegates from the gnomes, elves, dwarfs, and humans. The representatives of the Northern Alliance were the human factions, ogres, trolls, and orcs. Ambassador Runar was speaking about the importance of the organization toward defending world peace, particularly against the incursions from the north for the few last months.

"General Snagtann, what assurances can you give us that these incidents would not recur?" Ambassador Runar asked. "Your people have been a signatory to the charter in which you have agreed to work for peace, have you not?"

Prince Maura stood up and yelled, "Objection! I know very well of our obligations to this organization. Your statements are unwise and untrue."

Ambassador Runar motioned to the prince to sit down. "What is untrue of the allegations, sire?"

"With all due respect, sire, you cannot produce a single person to back up your claims. We have a right and a duty to patrol our borders. There may have been isolated instances, but there was never any intent to violate your lands," interjected the general.

Ambassador Runar knew that what he said was true. He also knew that the council would never administer any sanctions due to the in-fighting within the Southern Alliance. But he knew he was just buying time for Anthony and Amber. This meeting was a farce, and any attempt to thwart the desires of the north will end up in failure. Mortikon's plan was working. The human tendency to give in to lust and greed justified his plan. The human faction in the south was deeply fractured, and without adequate safeguards in place, many of them would defect to Mortikon.

It was now the fifteenth of April, and with another week of walking, they would be at Eldfjall, provided there would be no more delays. It was Amber who spotted the orc campsite about a mile away. Amber and Stemni hunkered down in a gully as Anthony clambered up the revetment to take a look. *This telescope was a great idea,* he thought as he scanned the area. What he saw stunned him. Thousands of orcs assembled, as if to deliver an assault upon some unsuspecting foe. He counted numbers of ogres and trolls in the camp. Scanning to the left, about three miles distance, he could hardly make out the huge broken Lava Gate. Turning back to the right, he could detect ballistae being towed by trolls. *Is this the dreaded assault from the north?* He espied scryers—dozens of them—with the fearful wraith riders in the skies above the camp. He scampered down and whispered, "We've got problems." He explained his what he saw. "Let us pray that the scryers and riders don't detect us. We've got about two hours of sunlight, so just hunker down till then. We'll work our way toward the mountain, give 'em wide berth after it gets dark." All of a sudden, Anthony fell to his knee, grabbing his head.

Anthony, I know you can hear me, said Mortikon. *I want that book. You have escaped without detection, and I applaud you for that. But the time is now running out. Give me the book and I will reward you handsomely.*

"Mortikon—he spoke to me," cried Anthony. "He wants the book, and our time is running out. Let's get out of here. I'll be glad when this is over."

It was now dark, and one more look at the foes ahead showed patrols in the vicinity of the camp. There were dozens of scryers with their conjured eyes in the skies overhead. The disembodied eyes were circling their creators like orangish orbs containing cat-eye-like things, scanning the landscape for anything out of the normal. Every now and then, they could hear the screeches from the wraiths gyrating above. "I've seen enough. Let's get out of here. I suggest we forgo the night rest. I want to put some distance between them and us," said Anthony. They trudged forward throughout the night without stopping. The scryers' eyes dissipated with every step they took. They neared the mountain slopes and turned toward the volcano. About ten more miles and they would reach it. The roiling, thunderous clouds seemed to thicken as they toiled onward. It appeared that the spinning clouds were being sucked into the volcano itself, burping out bolts of lightning to the skies. "One more rest stop. A short one at that," declared Anthony.

It was around noon when they stopped for a rest and grabbed a bite to eat. Stemni was enjoying a handful of wild mushrooms while the other two were eating flaxen bread. They had no other encounters with the orc raiding party, and they were engrossed with reaching the volcano. The winds had picked up considerably, but the ominous cloud cover from the volcano put a damper on their spirits.

With no warning other than the humming sword that Anthony bore, the party was pelted with boulders by a yeti! Growling and slobbering, a yeti stood on a ledge above, hurling huge stones at them. The creature must have been twice the size of Anthony.

Stemni was knocked unconscious as a boulder bounced off his head. Anthony yelled and charged the huge beast, which bared its fangs, ready to eat anything it could find. Amber cocked her arms and swung her daggers, which flew through the air. The yeti, armed with razor-sharp claws and fangs, leapt forward, arms flailing. Anthony's sword glistened in the sunlight as it tried to find its mark.

Amber joined in the fray. Her daggers drew blood from the beast as it howled in pain. Anthony's sword parried a sweep of its claws, drawing blood. Again and again, Amber sunk her daggers into the soft, blood-soaked fur. The stench from the beast was horrible. Anthony, with a leaping motion, silenced the monster with his sword, striking a blow to its heart.

"Stemni!" cried Amber as she rushed to help the little goblin. Anthony withdrew his sword, then plunged it again into the beast to be sure it was dead. Amber was holding Stemni's head in her lap when Anthony arrived, and he began to use his healing powers to slow down the bleeding.

"Well, he's not dead. Grab some mage bandages, would you?" instructed Anthony. "He can't walk, so I guess I have to carry him. Poor thing, he probably never saw it coming." After bandaging Stemni's wounds, Amber said, "Let's get out of here. We don't know how many are still around. We can't take more than two at a time. Here, I'll help with carrying him."

Anthony sighed and said, "You're right about that. I'll try to do some healing once we get out of here. So much for expediting the rest of the way. We still have about eight miles to go."

The two of them and the one wounded goblin was unexpected. Stemni was a heavy weight as the group trudged toward their destination. They had to stop several times to rest, with Stemni groaning every now and then. It must have been five o'clock, and the sun was setting, so they found a ravine to camp out but they made no fire. They were too close to the end of their journey. Anthony used his healing powers again, and Stemni seemed to get better. "Tomorrow will be the day," muttered Anthony.

They took turns over watching Stemni. They both had taken a liking to the little guy. With his head in bandages, he was a strange creature to look at. He would occasionally take a deep breath and let out a snore. It started to rain—mist, really—but they didn't care. They just wanted the task at hand to end. *Surely, Traikon will take pity on the miserable creature,* thought Anthony. When the group woke up, there was Stemni, sitting up. Amber was all smiles when she greeted the ailing goblin. "I am so glad that you are up and about. We had a scare from you yesterday. Look, over there," said Amber. "There's the volcano. Do you remember much from yesterday?"

Stemni had a blank look on his face and said, "No. Me head hurt."

She laughed and added, "Well, we had to kill a yeti, but we fixed him up real good too."

Anthony chuckled and said, "Well, don't take the bandages off yet. But I think you will be just fine. Might have a headache for a day or two though."

The end of the last leg of the journey was within sight. Before them lay Eldfjall, looming over them as a conquering beast, the volcano that had been there for a millennium. "Now to scale this monster and be done with it," said Anthony to Amber. Occasional ash and hot rock spewed from its mouth; the stench of sulfur was overpowering. Stemni was reluctant to go up, but he had no choice. "I follow you," said the green goblin. They started to climb the face of the volcano and it was tough going. Between falls from the loose gravel and ash, they would gain ten feet and lose four. Then there were the footholds and handholds that gave way because of their weight. It took about four hours of slipping and dodging rocks that were dislodged by the volcano's tremors before they reached a safe ledge where they rested for a bit. Looking down, they could view the landscape through which they had marched in their quest. Looking up, they could see what appeared to be a cave, or an apparition of a cave. Perhaps it was a way into the volcano. A belch emitted from the behemoth, showering them with debris.

"At this rate, we should near its entrance in about two more hours," shouted Anthony over the crash of thunder emitted from the volcano's mouth. Pressing on, the undaunted trio continued to climb the steep slopes. Having reached the entrance to the cave, they paused for a moment to relish the feat. "Now to find that Traikon character," boasted Anthony.

Traikon, the Savior

Finally, they had reached their destination. But what lay ahead? What destiny awaits them? They crept into the entrance not knowing whether before them would be a demon as what they had been told or his human form. With bated breath, they skulked along a passageway that reeked of sulfur fumes. And it was getting hot in there; they were sweating profusely as they neared the molten pit just ahead. The hot air in the passageway was stinging their lungs, making breathing difficult. As the group neared the precipice, Anthony said to Amber and Stemni, "Wait here," and advanced toward the crag. With the knapsack containing the book in hand, Anthony seemed to hesitate, turning toward Amber and Stemni.

Anthony, heed my call. Bring the book to me. With you at my side, we can rule the world! Bring the book, join me, and I will reward you with anything you desire, commanded Mortikon.

Amber was growing anxious as she suspected that Anthony was talking to Mortikon. Anthony's reluctance to cast the knapsack into the volcano was evident.

"Throw it in the volcano!" screamed Amber. "Throw it!" she pleaded. "For the love of god, destroy it!"

Yes, I detect you have had a change of heart! Yes, bring me the book, said Mortikon, softening his command.

"Mortikon, I have reached a decision. Rule the world, you say? Like the peons and down-and-out people in the slums of HearthGlen? NEVER! I cherish my freedom!" shouted Anthony to Mortikon. With that, Anthony heaved the knapsack into the lava beneath them.

"*NOOOO!*" screamed Mortikon as the knapsack sank below the molten lava.

Suddenly from the abyss below, the flapping of wings emerged from the molten magma.

Rising out of the steam and gushing molten rock appeared a dragon. It was a huge dragon with stubby arms and two horrific legs. It was an orange-red-colored dragon with a slithering tongue drooping from its mouth. Stemni cowered in fear against the cavern walls as Amber stood agog of the beast. In its grasp was the book, which was now covered in a blue glow.

"You have fulfilled your destiny, Anthony. You have chosen wisely, my child."

"Are you Traikon?" commanded Anthony. "Are you another minion of Mortikon?" He wrapped a hand upon the grip of his sword, ready to do battle. The dragon disappeared in a puff of smoke and what stood before Anthony was a human form.

"You need no weapon in your hand. I am Traikon, at your service. How can we ever thank you for your deeds of honor, righteousness, and courage?" asked Traikon.

Anthony withdrew his hand from his weapon and said, "But the book isn't destroyed. I was told to destroy it."

Traikon smirked and said, "The book can't be destroyed. The lava below is the only place where it will be safeguarded from the humans and Mortikon. As long as Eldfjall lives, no one can retrieve it. But there will be a time when another Anthony will heed the call—someone brave enough to do battle with the evil forces in the world."

"You asked how we can be thanked. Return Stemni to his true family, that is all that I wish," replied Anthony.

Traikon smiled and said, "But of course. Tut-tut, surely you desire a reward?"

Anthony thought for a moment and said, "Return us to our own world and time. I have some scores to settle there."

"As you wish," responded Traikon, "but let me give you a small gesture of payment." And with that, Traikon gave Anthony two bejeweled golden rings. "Wear them with pride. You will always be connected with us." He then summoned up a portal saying, "May the gods be with you."

Amber was on the verge of tears as she was going to miss Stemni, but she knew they were doing the right thing. With that, waving their hands in a gesture of good-bye, they stepped into the portal.

KAfLI:

ePISODe THREE

Anthony and Amber are back in their own time, having fulfilled Anthony's destiny. But the tale doesn't end here. They decided to join the rebel forces allied against Barry and his administration. Their taste for freedom was now unquenchable, and everything that had transpired encouraged them to become warriors. Because of their months-long experienced in the past, they were imbued with the attributes of honesty, courage, and righteousness. Never again will they be the subjects of tyranny, not from Barry and Janet Lygari nor Mortikon. They vowed to be true keepers of the spirits of the little people.

They were changed persons. Everything they believed from their childhoods had been smashed beyond repair. They made a promise to each other that when their children were born, they would be raised as elves. Amber also agreed that Agnar's lineage should never be broken. With the coming new generations, they would never fear Mortikon or his minions again.

They were transported back to their own time, to Blesugrof, the homestead of Anthony's ancestors.

Blesugrof, Home of the Brave

Blesugrof welcomed Anthony and Amber with artillery fire. Dust and shrapnel was everywhere with the sounds of explosions. On the hilltop where they were teleported to, they could see hundreds of rebels fleeing from the artillery bombardment. The artillery batteries had found their marks as wounded revolutionaries were being dragged back to their sanctuary. They ran as fast as they could toward the lone brick building where the wounded men had sought shelter. Out of breath, they reached the building. Out of the range of the artillery shells, Anthony and Amber began to assist those in need. *Great, out of the pan into the fire,* thought Anthony. He started using his healing powers on the most seriously wounded men first, while Amber helped other wounded mutineers to safety. There were men who were missing arms or legs, bathed in gore, or just screaming out of pain. No one was talking except to ask where they were hit. They were exposing wounds to see how bad they were injured and administrate triage. For hours, Anthony was using his healing powers, going from one wounded soldier to the next. He had to rest between the every third patient while his mana replenished itself. But there were scores of mangled bodies and wounded men to treat. Eventually the numbers of the wounded decreased as the artillery fire decreased too, allowing a much needed rest.

"Are you a doctor or what?" a stranger approached and asked. "How in the world do you do this? I didn't see any medicine, no scalpels or nothing."

"I'm no doctor," replied Anthony. He didn't want to explain it. "Just some home remedies from my mother."

"Well, I saw what you did, and it is a miracle. That's what I saw. Wounded men are up and about like they never got wounded," declared the stranger. "Where did you come from? I've never seen you here before. I'm Adam by the way, the group commander."

"I'm Anthony, Adam. Can I rest a bit before I answer any questions?" asked Anthony.

Adam smiled and said, "Sure thing, pal. What you have done here is going to make history. I'll check back with you later."

Amber bent down and whispered, "You better have a good story to tell." She laughed.

Adam sent a messenger to Anthony and Amber to meet him and a group of leaders to discuss their role in the organization. Adam seemed suspicious toward them, demanding who they were and how they came to be there.

"Like I said yesterday, we're from HearthGlen. I'm an archaeologist, and Amber here is my assistant," stated Anthony.

"How did you get here though? Seems like your responses are kinda vague. How did you get out of HearthGlen? Everyone needs papers to travel. Now, let's try it again," demanded Adam.

"If you think we are spies or working for the regime, forget it, buddy," interjected Amber.

Suddenly, Leo, the old man from the hotel, showed up. He approached with a hand extended, saying, "Well, Anthony, Amber, fancy meeting you here." Leo smiled.

Adam greeted Leo warmly and asked, "Do these two people know you?"

"But of course, of course. You're the newlyweds from Sanctuary City," said Leo to Amber.

"Wait a minute. You claim to be from HearthGlen, but you were in Sanctuary City?" demanded Adam suspiciously.

"Tut-tut there, Adam. I'll vouch for them. We survived a bombing in the café. They went to Sanctuary City on a honeymoon," advised Leo to Adam.

"O-okay. But how did you get here in the midst of a battle then?" inquired Adam. Still suspicious, he was waiting for a reply.

"Well, it seems that we got caught up in the revolution there. We needed to get out of the city as I was doing a dig site near Vokva," responded Anthony. "The rebel forces helped us escape the city."

"Well, we gotta be careful. Spies and such. Are you sure, Leo, that they are trustworthy?" inquired Adam.

"On my honor, these are worthy of my confidence in them," responded Leo to Adam.

"Now, Adam, what plans are you initiating after the barrage put a damper on things?" asked Leo to Adam.

"Excuse me, but I'm new here, and as much as I want to help, won't we need more men if you plan to attack Fort Hermana? The artillery and mortar pits will chew you up," advised Anthony.

"Well, we took the POL site out yesterday, and without air assaults from the drones, we tried to get closer to the fort. Reinforcements are out of the question as the trains have been put out of commission, so the regime can't send any help. Now if we can only take out the mortar pits and artillery, then we only have to blow the fence to get in," explained Adam.

"Well, that settles it then," said Amber, "We can help. A lot."

Anthony and Amber pulled Leo aside and thanked him for helping out with the interrogation by Adam. "We can take down the fencing around the city. We can take out the mortar pits too. We need a diversion. Fake an attack so the artillery will train on them. Withdraw, then do it again. The artillery fire can't lower their howitzers, so they can only shoot over our heads. It is the mortar pits that I'm worried about. Once the fence is down, we can enter the city and destroy the pits. We need a small group. Once we have an opening and get a foothold within the city, THEN we're in business. How many supporters do we have within the city?"

"Brilliant plan," replied Leo. "I think a lot of sympathizers are inside the city now. More than you think as the regime is hated. But how do you plan to get close enough to the fence? The machine gun emplacements and the mortar pits—we've already lost many men yesterday."

"Leave it to us. I need lots of explosives, satchel charges, grenades, ammo, and machine guns. We can make a supply depot closer to the fort. Like I said, we only need maybe seven men to carry our supplies," responded Amber.

"Oh, one more thing: can you talk to Adam about the plan? I, uh . . . how can I explain it? If you see things, or not see things, we, uh . . . have powers, like my healing powers. Don't blab about it, especially with Adam," requested Anthony.

It took weeks to set up their munitions for the supply depot; they had to hoard in different locations to ensure that if one was blown up, then they could get supplies from the next spot. It was working as planned. They would feint an attack and withdraw, then do it again. It was a simple plan, but an effective one, to fake attacks and draw fire away from Anthony's party. There were some wounded men, but nothing like before the couple had arrived. Soon the hard part would come: getting into the city itself. If the plan was successful, it could be used against the other cities of the administration.

Leo had done his job; Adam asked no questions of the newcomers. Adam's suspicions about Anthony and Amber were unfounded, and his attitude toward them changed. Anthony though had a funny feeling about Leo. How did a wealthy businessman, an older gentleman, get involved with the rebel forces? He seemed to be a leader of some kind, but not as a soldier. Something about Leo made him different, but he couldn't put a finger on it. Amber felt it too but brushed it aside.

Assault on Fort Hermana

Some people would look back on the assault of Fort Hermana as the turning point for the struggles of the freedom-loving rebels. With the walls breached, it wasn't long before the foothold became a surge of insurgents. Of course, everyone knew that Anthony and Amber were the true heroes of Fort Hermana. There were tales of heroic hand-to-hand fighting as the rebels tried to evict the regime in house-to-house struggles. There were many who had perished in the battles, many more were wounded. For days, the battle raged as many sympathizers came out into the open streets and joined in kicking the regime out. It seemed that some of them were turncoats, doffing their FBI, DHS, or TSA uniforms in exchange for civilian clothing. On the fifth day, the old fort had been liberated, and the flag of the rebels flew over the city. Strangely, the emblem on the new flag was a dragon. Everyone was dancing in the streets, kissing each other, and acting like they were long-lost childhood friends. Of course, in the south, the news spread like wildfire. The egregious members of the administration were scrambling to leave or hide, like rats abandoning a sinking ship. It took a few more months before most of the large metropolis fell; there was only HearthGlen left.

Anthony and Amber was summoned to the old DHS building, renamed Freedom Hall, where they were to be honored for helping with the liberation of the city. Everyone from Blesugrof was there, cheering and applauding their new heroes. Adam gave an excellent speech lauding both Anthony and Amber. Sitting next to him was Leo. Guest speakers talked about their exploits during the final days and how many were still alive because of Anthony and Amber.

It was now time for Anthony and Amber to speak. Anthony spoke of the honor, chivalry, courage, and righteousness of each person in the room. He choked up a few times as he was close to tears. Amber took over, and she spoke of freedom. In the end, she wanted to thank everyone for believing in them, and said that all they wanted to do now was to go to their new home, Blesugrof. There was a time for war and a time for peace, and now they only wished that they would not be viewed us as heroes but rather friends.

The applause was deafening and well-earned as they left the stage. Anthony whispered to Amber, "I used be a mouse of a man, a nothing, a loser. Thank you for believing in me." He kissed her. Backstage, Adam relinquished the title for Blesugrof, all one hundred hectares, and said, "You've earned this." Anthony and Amber sought Leo out as he was leaving the building, and Leo said, "The land of Blesugrof has finally been returned to its original owners."

"W-what do you mean by that?" asked a puzzled Anthony. "W-who are you?"

Leo replied, "Dost thou not know, my son?" as he vanished into thin air.

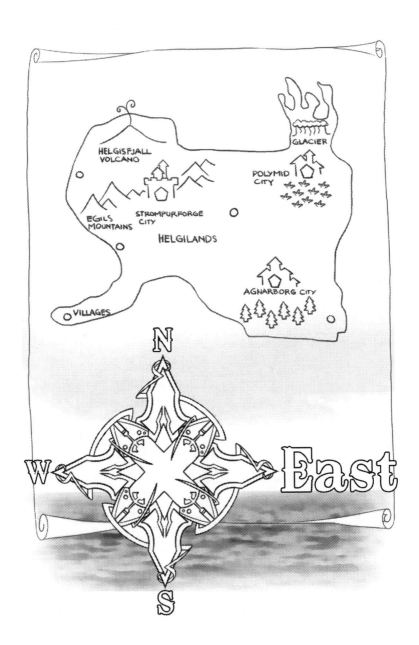

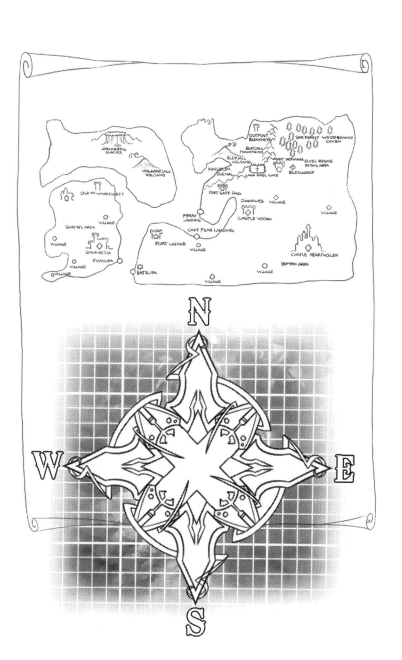